W9-AWQ-565

FEVER

FEVER

A NOVEL BY

SEAN ROWE

LITTLE, BROWN AND COMPANY
NEW YORK   BOSTON

Copyright © 2005 by Sean Rowe

All rights reserved. No part of this book may be reproduced in any form or by any electronic or mechanical means, including information storage and retrieval systems, without permission in writing from the publisher, except by a reviewer who may quote brief passages in a review.

Little, Brown and Company
Time Warner Book Group
1271 Avenue of the Americas, New York, NY 10020
Visit our Web site at www.twbookmark.com

First Edition: September 2005

The characters and events in this book are fictitious. Any similarity to real persons, living or dead, is coincidental and not intended by the author.

Library of Congress Cataloging-in-Publication Data
Rowe, Sean.
    Fever / Sean Rowe. — 1st ed.

        p.   cm.
    ISBN 0-316-01174-6
    1. Cruise ships — Fiction. 2. Miami (Fla.) — Fiction. 3. Robberies — Fiction. 4. Hostages — Fiction. 5. Cuba — Fiction. I. Title.
PS3618.O8735F48   2005
813'.6 — dc22

                                                            2005002588

10 9 8 7 6 5 4 3 2 1

Q-MART

Printed in the United States of America

for
Tom & Jan

PART ONE

FIRE

I

"SOME GUYS DON'T KNOW when to quit. That's your problem."

It was Fontana's voice. I heard the voice before I felt the hand on my shoulder. When I looked up he was standing behind me, hazy in the smoked glass of the mirror on the back bar, out of prison three years early.

"You think you've seen it all," he said, the hand gone. "You think you've run your course, but you can't quite bring yourself to cash it in. So on you go: another day, another drink. What you really need is to find some noble exit. Some way of going out in a big blaze of glory."

The kid behind the bar had been filling sample glasses and letting me taste each one. The place made its own beer: raspberry, India pale ale, one that tasted like molasses. You could see big copper vats behind a glass wall.

"Let's grab a table outside," Fontana said. "You have to get out in the sun, or what's the point? This is Miami."

When I got up he was already walking out to the patio, wind catching his jacket. I couldn't see if he was carrying.

"Check it out," he said when we were sitting down.

I thought he meant the girl on the Jet Ski, but he was looking at a rust-bucket freighter coming toward us down Government Cut. The harbor pilot went on ahead. A tug stayed behind the pilot boat, slaloming through the chop, dragging the freighter backward out the ship channel.

Fontana put on a pair of sunglasses. He had binoculars with him: civilian ones, out of a sporting goods store.

"You could drop that baby in the mouth of the channel and shut down this whole city for a week," he said, looking at the freighter. "Three days, anyway. The cargo port. The river. Half the cruise ships in North America."

I didn't know if we were bumping into each other or it was something else. He picked up the field glasses, and I caught a flash of holster leather underneath his jacket.

"You'd have to make sure it swung sideways," I offered. "Before you blew it."

"Or after." He put down the binoculars. "How you

liking retirement, Matthew? Or I guess it's semiretirement?"

"Fine. Same as you, right?"

"I don't think so. Anyway, that's not what I hear."

"No?"

The freighter was passing us now, about sixty yards from the patio. A woman at a table nearby was showing a little boy how to wave. There was a man on the freighter's bridge in a white shirt with blue epaulettes on the shoulders. The man dragged on a cigarette. I got one out myself.

"So you're living down here again?"

"It's a great town," he replied, not exactly an answer.

I looked at him the way you do with people, trying to get a good, full look when you think they won't catch you doing it. He was thinner, and I could understand why he wanted to be outside: he was very pale. I noticed caps on a couple of teeth.

"How long you been out?"

"Three weeks and three days," he said, taking off his sunglasses and cleaning them with a napkin.

"How was it?"

He blew on his glasses and kept rubbing. "How was it? That's a great question, Matt. Well, let me see: how was it. Do you know what a blanket party is?"

"I've heard the term. What do you say we just drop it?"

"They bring you down the cell block the first day, all the way down and back up the other side, their version of a perp walk. Then they open the door of a holding cell and in you go. All the cons are waiting to meet you. It's the neighborhood welcoming committee. A couple guys stand up, taking their time. They hold a blanket in front of the bars, and the next thing you know, another one of 'em gets around behind you and hits you with something sneaky, maybe a soup can stuck in a sock. You go down, and that's when the fun begins. They take turns with you, Matt, that's what they do, three or four guys holding you down with a towel stuck in your mouth, everyone else helping out and taking turns. That's a blanket party."

He finished with his glasses and put them back on. "I'm trying to think what else I can tell you about being a defrocked drug agent in a state penitentiary. I caught up on my knitting?"

"I'm going to order a drink," I said, and I did. I thought about the bottle of Advil in my desk drawer at work. My hand ached, worse than it had in weeks.

"One hell of a current in there at the change of tide," Fontana was saying. "Especially an autumn tide. Mix it up with a new moon, you got a doozy. That's why that tug's straining like it is."

I looked, and he was right.

"The way to do it is wait till the freighter's right between the jetties, the narrowest point. You do it with some dynamite in the bow, say fifteen pounds. Nothing fancy. Dynamite and sandbags, a directed charge. You blow a hole in the port bow; it swings the whole ship around. Kid stuff."

"You need a hobby."

He laughed. "What I hear is you like to drink a fifth of Maker's Mark a day and hang out in titty bars. Is that a hobby?"

I shrugged. "It's a free country."

"Yeah? You should turn on CNN sometime. You got survivalist militias, you got whacked-out religious cults, you got kids with purple hair running around calling themselves antiglobalists. They don't think it's a free country. The whole thing makes me glad I'm out of law enforcement. Maybe you should get out too."

He couldn't leave the binoculars alone. He had picked them up again, taking off his glasses to squint through them. He said, "You could get some serious action in this town, come to think of it. Your old buddies at the Bureau are scared shitless these Cubans are going to get serious someday, actually do something instead of screaming at each other on AM radio and shaking their fists at Castro."

"I wouldn't know."

"I thought you out-to-pasture FBI guys all stayed in touch, had cocktail parties."

I let it slide. It was a nice afternoon, cool for October and a little windy. Fishing boats were scattered all over the channel, a regular traffic jam. I felt sorry for the harbor pilot. Not too sorry, of course; those guys have a hell of a union. I could see the stern of the freighter now. In a few minutes the ship would be heading out to sea. The waitress brought my drink.

"I been playing with this thing," Fontana said. He had slipped on a pair of calfskin gloves. I looked down, and there was a little black gizmo on the table. "Try it out. You'll get addicted. A friend of mine, his sister's kid turned me on to it."

There was a screen, like on a pager. The thing was the size of a cigarette pack, with a dull metal casing, and when I picked it up, it was heavier than I had thought it would be. I wasn't big on games.

"You push the button on the side to start it up," he said.

I did. Nothing happened. Then the screen lit up and displayed little green letters. The little green letters said, *Bang!*

Right then I knew what was going to happen next but I didn't even have time to breathe.

The explosion ripped through the patio like a gust of wind. Someone in one of the fishing boats was yelling, "*¡Coño! ¡Coño! ¡Coño!*" Everyone was screaming. On the wooden deck, on my stomach, I looked out from between two balusters and saw the freighter in flames. It had swung sideways in the channel, nose down and sinking fast. A guy on the tugboat was going nuts, trying to get the lines loose. He gave up and dove overboard, and the tug capsized.

Fontana was still sitting in his chair. He was laughing, sipping my drink. "This is great," he said. He got up, giving his jacket a little hitch.

"You owe me one," he added, "and this is it, some of it, anyway. Let's not forget who could have been sitting in that eight-by-twelve up at Raiford the last three years instead of me. I'm at the Delano. You feel like it, give me a call. I got something going on I'd like to include you in."

He gave the gizmo a glance. It was under the table next to my foot, or had been; now I didn't see it. "You know, Matthew, a man can go his whole life in this country and never know if he's a coward. You want a blaze of glory? I'm going to serve it to you on a silver fucking platter."

He laughed again and walked inside. No one paid attention to him. After another minute I got up and sat in the chair and finished my drink, thinking to slip the black box in my pocket.

I reached down for it and froze. I shoved the table aside. The deck underneath was empty.

"The Vanishing Jack" was Fontana's favorite card trick from years ago. He would do it so fast you hardly saw his hands move.

2

THE NEXT MORNING it was all over the front page of the *Herald*. Hector came in around eight thirty, sat with one leg over the chair arm in my office, and read the whole thing out loud. Especially the letter.

The letter called Castro the Antichrist and also had some choice words for Congress, for gutting the travel embargo. The idea was that Cuban hard-liners in Miami had blown up the freighter as a warning. Bigger trouble was promised if the United States didn't do some soul-searching and reimpose full trade sanctions against Havana, cut off diplomatic ties, make the ballet dancers and boxers stay home. An exile's pipe dream.

And that's what made the letter perfect: the delusion. It hit every note, right down to the spelling mistakes. It was signed the October 28th Brigade. Today was Thursday, October 29.

"What do you think?" Hector asked. The kid was playing it cool.

"I think someone better get the channel open or we're both out of a job."

The Corps of Engineers had a two-thousand-ton barge crane on its way down from Titusville. Meanwhile thirty freighters were backed up in Lagarre Anchorage off Miami Beach, waiting to get into port. The inbound cruise ships were being diverted to Port Everglades and Port Canaveral, but the larger problem was the six luxury liners trapped in their berths at Dodge Island, each one bigger than a football field. The Italians at Costa Cruises had already tried to run the *Majesty of the Waves* through Cape Florida Channel and gone aground.

At noon I was going to meet at the port director's office with people from the three top cruise lines. Tanel, the big man in our outfit, was flying in from Chicago with a couple of board members, and right now I wanted to get rid of Hector. On the other hand, he was a good weather vane.

"What do *you* think?" I asked.

He shrugged. "It could be a hoax. It could be an insurance scam, or some kind of business payback. The freighter was docked on the river. Those guys on the river are animals. It's a fight to the death up there."

"But you don't think so."

"No," he said, heating up. "This thing with Cuba, there had to be some kind of backlash. I mean, it's the final betrayal, right? You start with Kennedy and the Bay of Pigs and end up with Congress queering the Helms-Burton Act. There was a rumor downtown a couple of days ago that Castro was getting invited to the White House for dinner."

Another pipe dream. I wondered if Hector believed it or if he was just bringing it up as a sample of local gossip.

"Oh boy." I acted like I'd thought of something. "I need you to take Neal and do a walk-through on the *Ecstasy*. Not the passenger areas, just the chandler bays. Look for anything out of the ordinary. New trucks, people you don't recognize. Get the purser to go over the provisions manifest. Tell him I said so."

"OK, chief. You want me to leave the newspaper?"

Hector called me "chief" whenever he got excited. The last time was in June after one of the cabin stewards raped a passenger on the *Stargazer*. I had a sudden image of Hector and Neal Atlee beating him with chopped-off pool cues behind a stack of ship containers, the floodlights from the gantries shining down on wet asphalt. Afterward, we put the steward on a plane back to Malaysia. The company settled out of court with the girl's parents, which was routine, but this time the price tag was high six figures. Things had been pretty quiet since Labor Day.

I told Hector to take his paper with him, and I tried to get ready for the meeting. Dolores brought in a list of employees hired in the last three months. The officers were all Svens and Larses. The crew was mostly Filipino, some South Americans. While I went through the list I called Paul Lewis at the North Miami field office, expecting to get his voice mail. He picked up and said, "Well, well. Loose Cannon Shannon."

"Paul. I hate to trouble you, but I've got a sit-down in three hours with the port director and Tanel and the whole Supreme Soviet down here."

"I know. I'm invited."

"I wasn't aware."

"I'm supposed to assure you guys that the FBI has a serious hard-on for the bomber. Which we do. The way I know is I've got nine agents on loan from Atlanta camped out in the bull pen. None of them speak any Spanish, of course. I'm going to say your people are supposed to keep their eyes peeled for suspicious characters, like guys carrying Cuban flags and tote bags full of dynamite."

I decided not to ask about the dynamite. Then I wondered. The newspaper hadn't said a word about dynamite. It was a detail that had been held back from the press. So why would Lewis mention it? It was exactly the kind of thing I would have thrown out as bait, just to see who nibbled. Or who didn't. But now it was too late to bite.

"You think this is for real?"

"It doesn't matter what I think," he said. "The lab has the letter that was sent to the *Herald,* I'm not telling you anything you wouldn't know anyway. Maybe forensics in Washington can do something with it. Meanwhile we beat the bushes."

"They're going to want me to run my own investigation. I can smell it coming."

Lewis laughed. "Not a good idea."

"I know. I was thinking you could mention that to Tanel."

"I'm getting the picture," he said. "By the way, how much they paying you over there, Matt?"

"A lot," I said, lying. "You're coming up on your twenty-five, aren't you?"

"You got that right."

"What's your plan?"

"Go somewhere with trout and forget I met the human race. I've got to run. See you at noon."

• • •

TANEL MADE A STEEPLE out of his fingers and said, "I think at this juncture we'd all like to hear from our director of security."

The eyes swung my way, the chairs squeaking. Tanel was Israeli, but he was going through a big English-gentleman phase. All the chairs were burgundy leather. I expected pictures of fox hunts on the walls any day now. The English-gentleman phase included Mary, and Tanel was in the bad habit of bringing her to meetings to serve drinks. Today she wore slacks that were like riding pants, and a tweed jacket. She set a glass of Scotch in front of Tanel. The rest of us were drinking coffee or fizz water. I had to hand it to the old guy, he didn't give a shit. One in the afternoon, and he was on his third double.

"I'll start with what we know," I began. "We've got a hundred-and-ninety-foot bulk cargo trader owned by Poseidon Transport sunk at the mouth of the ship channel. It'll be up and out in seventy-two hours, maybe sooner. Until then we've got a logistical —"

"Nightmare," said Tanel. "You can go ahead and say it, Matt."

A little joke from the big man. He was looking at the ceiling now, swiveled back from the conference table with his fingers laced behind his neck.

"Right," I said. "Some real challenges."

"We already know that. Do you think this is terrorism?"

"I don't know. In a sense it's irrelevant. The thing to do at this stage is take precautions, which we're doing." I wanted to back up a little. I waited to see if I had the floor. "We've got a blown-up freighter and a letter in the *Herald* that may or may not be authentic. Let's keep in mind there's been no loss of life."

"But that's just by happenstance, now isn't it?"

Tanel again, the debate team captain.

"Hard to say."

This time I gave it a good long pause, to be sure I had settled his hash. I was planning to touch on the cancellations the marketing guy had just gone over, maybe repackage some of Paul Lewis's speech. Lewis had left ten minutes earlier with the Italians and the people from Trinity, the number two line. It was just the big boys now and the port director and some of his staff. Fuck it, I thought, here we go.

"Of course, the sixty-four-thousand-dollar question is

could this happen to a Festival Cruise Lines vessel, and the answer is yes. In fact, it could be the next logical step: bomb a recognizable, highly visible cruise ship with two thousand tourists on board."

They were paying attention.

"If," I said, "this was a Hezbollah or Qaeda hit, or some domestic antigovernment group. But there's no reason yet to believe it was. Let's assume for the moment the letter is real. OK. What we're dealing with is a bunch of serious Castro haters, local Cubans. They're not extortionists for money, they're extortionists for glory. They want Washington to say, '*Sí, señor*. We will close down trade routes again.' They want to make trouble, but they don't want to completely alienate the authorities, and they certainly don't want to piss off local right-wingers, because that's where the glory is going to come from. In the end they want to be good Americans. They want to be good boys. They want Mama to pat them on the head. It's a matriarchal culture."

One of the staffers giggled. Earlier I had seen her staring at my hand the way I imagined she would stare at something unexpected and skittering in a damp bathtub or beneath the lid of a water-meter housing. The tension at the corners of her mouth was half fear and half fascination, and she had dropped her eyes as soon as I met her gaze. She was quite a looker, and I remembered hearing she was recently divorced, but even thinking about that seemed like a lot of trouble.

"So much for speculation," I continued. "What we're doing at the moment is tightening security with our shoreside suppliers because that's the likeliest avenue for a bomb to get smuggled onto a cruise ship. We're reviewing recent employment records. And a few other things."

"Any more thoughts?" Tanel asked.

"That about gets it."

"Well, Matt," he said, two fingers thumping the rim of his rocks glass, "I think there's a lot more you can do."

Here it comes, I thought.

"I think it would be a good idea for you to initiate your own investigation," he said.

"Of the freighter bombing."

"Of the freighter bombing." His hand was a claw clutching the glass, all blue veins and bone.

Mary poured some coffee in my cup. I caught the scent of jasmine as she moved away.

"Based on what I've heard here today, the local FBI field office seems to be handling that," I said. "I think it's a bad idea to parallel their efforts."

"You have a distinct advantage. The FBI is looking out for the welfare of the nation. You're only looking after the interests of the world's largest cruise line. And you can afford to be" — he hesitated here, giving the Scotch a swirl — "a bit less formal in your approach. What do you say, Mary?"

Tanel reached behind him to grab her arm but missed. Mary stopped where she had been walking past and looped her arms around the chair to put her hands on his lapels, smiling out at the conference table.

"What do you say we give Mr. Shannon a little encouragement?" Tanel said.

She looked down at him, right on cue. She brushed her hair back behind one ear and cooed: "That sounds *marvelous,* darling."

"I think I heard you call this the sixty-four-thousand-dollar question," Tanel said, looking up at Mary but talking to me. "Let's say we'll make that your bonus when you introduce Mr. Antonopoulos to the mad bomber." Antonopoulos was the operations manager. Right now he was looking up from some papers trying to figure out if he was supposed to laugh. The port director was doing a good job of staring at nothing from behind his over-size, indoor-outdoor sunglasses. Tanel sat straight up in his chair, one hand palm down on the conference table. He was looking at me, eyes like stones in a mountain stream. "Of course," he said, "a Polaroid of the body would suffice. The mad bomber could sink to the bottom of the Atlantic, and this corporation wouldn't give a fiddler's fuck."

Then the smile came back, and he raised the glass to his lips.

This was something new. I had to say, it made things interesting.

3

THE DELANO stood on a narrow lot, but it was deep, all the way through from Collins to the beach. I paid the cabbie and got out. After I walked up the steps, and the doorman opened the door, I started to see what was what.

In front of me was a long, dim lobby, and it was crowded. Curtains billowed up to the ceiling. All the staff wore white.

I was early, so I decided to look around. The lobby turned into a restaurant that reminded me of New York, everyone wearing black or gray, the women with dark lipstick. Or that's the way it seemed in the low light. Then I was outside, next to the swimming pool.

A line of royal palms rose from either side of the

water. Hammocks swayed between some of them, and a full-length mirror in a wooden frame twinkled in the shadows. The mirror stood on the grass the way it would stand in a bedroom. A drunk guy was posing and puckering in front of it.

"Look at me!" he said, falsetto. "Look at *me!*" He stuck his ass out and wiggled it. A woman was with him, and she laughed. He was pretending to be a fashion model, and I could understand why. Coming through the lobby, I'd noticed quite a few of them.

I saw a tiki bar at the far end of the pool; a café table and two wrought-iron chairs stood in the water, an artistic touch. The pool was very shallow at that end, maybe three inches deep, and I wondered if any of the hotel guests ever waded out and actually sat at the table.

I got a beer from the kid at the tiki bar and started walking toward the other side of the pool. Two guys in their fifties and a young woman were up ahead, the men pushing the girl on a swing that hung from a gumbo-limbo tree. I could see she was something special. The men wore double-breasted suits, but the young woman looked like she had just stepped off a yacht. She was laughing. She wore a sort of silk skirt wrapped around her waist and tied on one side, and a bikini top. It was hard not to look at the bikini, so I slowed down and pretended to take a new interest in the swimming pool.

One of the men grabbed the ropes holding the swing and made it stop. He said something I couldn't hear, and the three of them moved off to one of the cabanas that lined that side of the pool. When they were inside, the white canvas curtain was pulled across the doorway.

I got close and heard the woman, and then I heard a slap. One of the men laughed. Then the other's voice said, "That's it, baby. Yes." There was nothing for a while. Then came a low moan, the girl. I moved under the shadow of a tree near the big mirror, catching a glimpse of myself. Because of the light, I almost didn't recognize the image. It could have been anybody.

The curtain pulled back, and the girl came out. She started walking down the path before she noticed me.

"Getting a thrill?" she asked.

"Whatever," I said. I didn't know what to say. I put my hand in my pocket to warm it up.

She walked past, and I watched her go to the bar. Soon she headed back with two glasses in her hands. I had lit a cigarette.

She came off the path and moved right up in front of me. She bent down, put the drinks on one of the flag-stones, and stood up, reaching behind her back to untie her top.

Her top fell to the ground. She looked at me while she massaged her breasts for a time; then she just stood there, arms at her sides. It was cold. Everyone was inside the hotel.

She put her top back on and said: "You're wondering what it costs."

"Yes," I answered. She was right. It was exactly what I had been thinking.

"That guy, the one with the beard. He owns a sugar mill in Belle Glade. He's worth seventeen million dollars. He pays me thirty thousand at the beginning of each fiscal quarter, and I suck his cock until the next installment."

I heard some low laughter from inside the cabana.

"Whereupon," she said, "I decide if I'm interested in doing it again."

"You could make the same thing modeling."

"No, I couldn't. They want anorexic children these days."

I really looked at her then. I put her at about twenty-five. She was beautiful.

"Twenty-eight," she said, reading me.

"Who's the other guy?"

"That's Tim," she said. "An out-of-town guest. We're entertaining. Any other questions?"

What the hell. It was what I really wanted to know. "What happens if a higher bidder shows up?"

"That's up to me. Entirely." She picked up the drinks.

She ran the tip of her tongue very slowly across her top lip. Then she turned back toward the white canvas.

• • •

It was just Fontana's style: the biggest suite in the hotel. I got off the elevator on the fifteenth floor and walked down the hall and knocked.

He pulled the door open, and everything was white. The walls were white. The carpet was white. There was a minibar, and it was white too. A sconce stuck out from the wall like you see in old paintings, but instead of a candlestick or a vase, it held a green apple.

Fontana was wearing Armani: black jacket, white trousers, no tie, but the pearl-gray shirt buttoned up to the neck. He had an unlit cigar in his left hand. I could hear voices coming from another room. "Matthew," he said, stepping back so I could walk in.

I followed him through an arched doorway into a sitting room, where he flopped on a white couch. I stopped, and the talk did too.

A little dark guy in a brown suit sat on a chair in the corner. I looked at the couch across from Fontana, and I was looking at Kip Purvis, half a lifetime later but almost exactly the same: same electric-blue eyes, same deepwater tan. The big difference was that his hair had turned completely white. He was pumped up from weight lifting, stretch marks around his neck and shoulders. A woman sat next to him. Kip jumped up and came at me, grinning.

"Holy shit!" he said, "I can't fucking believe this, man!" When he said it, the saliva made me flinch.

He gave me a bear hug, lifting me off the floor. He started shaking my hand and forgot to let go. He was shaking my hand, but he was also shaking.

"Krystal! This is Matthew Shannon!"

The woman stood up and did what's left of a curtsy in some parts of the South. She stuck out her hand, but I couldn't get to it across the coffee table, so she gave up and sat down, smiling. Krystal turned out to be Kip's sister.

"That's Rodríguez," Kip said. He pointed his thumb at the dark guy in the suit. "Fuck him."

Kip pounded me on the back for a while, then went to a countertop jammed with bottles and glasses. He fetched me a Negra Modelo and one for himself.

"Old times," he said, clicking his beer against mine.

Fontana was looking at me and smiling. I looked at Kip because anyone would. He had put the beer on the coffee table and started flexing his biceps like the Incredible Hulk, standing there in a red muscle shirt, blue jeans, and ostrich-skin Tony Lamas. The last time I'd seen him was in a safe house outside Thien Pao. One of the SEAL teams had fed him some acid, and after he took off his clothes and wouldn't stop screaming, we duct taped his mouth shut and handcuffed him to a water pipe. Later on he got court-martialed, I couldn't remember what for. I'd heard he was working in Guatemala, Africa before that.

"He's training for Mister Over Forty," Krystal explained. "The regional pose-off."

Fontana burst out laughing, and the dark guy went so far as to smile and hoist one ankle across his knee.

"Sit down, Matthew," Fontana suggested.

Kip winked at me and quit his strut. "Gotta water the weasel," he said and disappeared through the doorway.

Fontana lit his cigar. "Adam was walking through the Garden of Eden," he said, exhaling. "The clouds rolled back, and God looked down and said, 'How you liking it down there, Adam my boy?'"

I sat on the sofa next to Krystal. She was working on some needlepoint that involved ducklings and kittens.

"'Oh, I love it,' Adam answered. 'All the animals are so cuddly and friendly. The grass is so nice and green.' 'That's fine, Adam,' God says. 'But I'll make you a deal. I'm going to send you a new animal. This one's called a woman.'"

Fontana gazed through a cloud of blue smoke, a look

where you couldn't tell how far he was looking. He found something wrong with his cigar and started working on it with a little clipper he fished out of his pocket.

" 'She'll be your pal, help you out with any projects you got going,' " he said. " 'She'll smooth down the grass for you at night and make a nice warm bed, and she'll fulfill every one of your sexual fantasies. Not only that, she'll *invent* sexual fantasies you couldn't have dreamed up on your own.' "

"This is some joke?" It was the first peep out of the dark guy. He looked nervous, and I didn't blame him.

"Of course it's a joke, you fucking monkey," Kip said, coming back into the room and zipping his fly. "Shut up."

Fontana cleared his throat. He was ignoring them both, looking out the open doors to a balcony where the night breeze blew the curtains around.

"Adam scratches his head and says, 'Well, that's fine, God. But you said this was a deal. What's it going to cost me?' God says, 'An arm and a leg. Your left arm and your right leg.' Adam scratches his head again. Then he says: 'What could I get for a rib?' "

Dead silence. Then Krystal laughed and said, "I don't get it."

Fontana looked like he'd gone to sleep. After a minute he opened his eyes and got up and poured something complicated at the bar. Kip shrugged. The dark guy, Rodríguez, lit a cigarette, and he and I looked at each other.

I decided to have a smoke, too. I had pretty much figured out we were waiting for someone else to show up when a loud knock struck the door. Fontana disappeared into the next room and came back with a slim black guy. The guy was wearing a guayabera and a beret, looking like a tropical Black Panther.

Fontana sat down, and the black guy glared around the room.

"Billy Bryant," said Fontana.

It took me a minute, and then I remembered: Pan Am, 1978, Kennedy to Heathrow. And an armored car out West somewhere. Maybe more than one.

The guy went over to the far side of the room and sat on one of the chairs. He took off the beret and hung it on his knee. He put his arms behind his head, but he looked even stiffer than Rodríguez.

"Now that we're all here, Kip," Fontana said, "why don't you explain to your old army buddy what the plan is."

Kip giggled. Krystal looked up from her needlepoint and smiled.

"Matthew, ol' buddy ol' pal, we're gonna hijack a cruise ship," Kip said. "And not just any cruise ship. The

Norwegian Empress, pride of the Festival Cruise Lines fleet. One of yours."

"I'm outta here." It was the black guy, Bryant. He jumped up and took some steps past the couch and then stopped near the doorway. He wheeled around and whipped his arms out wide to make a point, flinging his beret by accident. It hit the wall, and Rodríguez jumped.

"Listen," Bryant said, going to get his hat, "I walk in here and here's this cat I never seen before, and next thing I know you're putting our business in the street? This guy could be anyone. He could be wired!" He looked me in the face for the first time. "I'm checking this man for a wire right now, or I'm outta here."

I was about to say don't bother, we'll leave together.

Fontana blew another cloud. "I've got an even better idea," he said. "Why don't we go for a ride?"

4

IT WAS ALL SIX of us in a Chevy Astro going across the causeway and down U.S. 1 until Kip pulled over and got out and refused to get back in until Fontana ditched the cigar. Fontana said he'd consider it and sat there in the front passenger seat of the minivan trying different stations on the radio, smoking. Kip stomped off across the parking lot.

I went into the Dixie Creme next door to get some coffee. Rodríguez came with me. I looked out the window and saw Kip with Krystal on his shoulders doing squats.

Rodríguez got his coffee and sat down at a booth. I sat in the booth across from his, facing the same way, toward the highway. It was very bright in the donut shop. When

I glanced at him, the little guy had his head in his hands, and his shoulders were shaking. Something made me look down at his shoes on the tile floor, and I thought, Jesus, they're just like mine. Which was to say: the last lace-up shoes in Miami. Come to think of it, the guy looked like a shoe salesman.

He was really sobbing. I could see Bryant sitting in the minivan's slid-open doorway with ten thousand cars going by on U.S. 1, smoking a joint. He was laughing at something Fontana said. Kip was doing push-ups.

Rodríguez was drying up a bit, poking at his eyes with a paper napkin. I waited a minute, then stuck out my hand, careful to keep looking straight ahead. You never knew how these Latins were going to react.

"Matthew Shannon," I said.

He coughed, and I felt him take my hand. He had a nice grip, like maybe he'd done some real work when he was younger.

"My name is Manuel Rodríguez Colón," he said. "Here you would call it Manny."

"Nice to meet you, Manny." I blew on my coffee. I couldn't think of the next thing to say. "I was thinking you looked like a shoe salesman."

"Eh?"

"Luces como un vendedor de zapato," I said.

"Ah."

"Where are you from?"

He thought that was funny.

"Colombia. Near Cali," he said. "I am sure you have heard of Cali."

"Yeah," I answered. "What's going on here, Manny?"

"Whadyou mean?"

"For instance, where are we going?"

I could feel him looking at me, so I glanced over.

"To the miniature warehouse," he said.

"OK. Well, let me ask you this. What's going on with you? How come you're so upset?"

"It has nothing to do with our negotiation." He meant the business at hand, I thought. *Negocio* means "business" in Spanish.

He shook his head, looking sad. I thought he was going to start up again. I tried to give him my napkin, but he wasn't paying attention. He was looking at the floor.

"You are wearing Florsheim Imperials," he commented. "The Cadillac of footwear."

And then I remembered: the shoes. I had seen him in the federal courthouse, in the hallway outside the central courtroom where they have the big mural behind the judge's bench that shows the history of Miami: fishermen and ocean liners and black guys with baskets of oranges; people in Roaring Twenties outfits getting off a

Flying Clipper down at Dinner Key. He was one of Fontana's confidential informants. But that must have been, what, four years ago?

"My father was a shoe salesman," he went on. "I myself was an accountant." He blew his nose. "I married a girl in my village."

Then he did start up again.

I lit a cigarette. "Hey, Manny? I know how it is, OK?"

He took a pause. "It is — complex."

I was watching a cop get out of a squad car and walk toward the donut shop.

"My brother-in-law, he thought I was not good enough for to marry his sister," Manny said. "I was working for him. For him, and for other people."

"Manny, right now let's just wander outside."

He grabbed my arm as I was getting up. His eyes were wild.

"For me it was just a business, like selling shoes. I was an accountant, a bookkeeper. But she was different. My wife. She became corrupted. Later, she went with other men."

The cop was coming through the door now, heading for the counter.

"I saw her two days ago!" Manny said. "Here in Miami! I could hardly recognize her. She was much younger than I when we married, but not now."

"Is that why you're mixed up in this? You're trying to get back at her? Or your brother-in-law?"

He thought that was hilarious. The cop looked over, leaning against the counter.

"My brother-in-law is dead. There is only one reason I am mixed up in this," he said, bitter, "which is to get free from your friend Mr. Jack Fontana."

I must have looked like I didn't believe him.

"Also the money." He smiled. "I have told you, I was an accountant."

Not anymore, I thought. You're an ex-accountant who's about to get himself in a shitload of trouble. An accountant who's too dumb to notice a cop in a uniform thirty feet away.

"Let's get in the van, Manny."

When we were out the door and halfway across the parking lot, he asked, "What explicitly will be your role in the operation?"

"I'm not involved in the operation."

He stopped. "So it is untrue what I have heard?"

"What have you heard, Manny?"

"That Mr. Jack Fontana went to prison in the place of you. That you have now a debit to repay."

He was letting me know he knew. That they all knew what I owed Fontana, maybe even how it had happened.

After he gave me a good, long look, Manny smiled and started walking again and climbed into the van.

We drove down U.S. 1, nobody talking. Then we turned onto a side street into a warehouse district with a long row of shop spaces, mechanics' bays with roll-up metal doors. Kip pulled up in front of one of them and got out. He fiddled with the lock and then ran the door up, letting the headlights flood the inside. As soon as he did, I wanted to run.

5

THE WAREHOUSE wasn't much bigger than a two-car garage. We walked inside while Fontana flipped on the overhead lights and rolled the door down behind us.

A pair of .50 caliber machine guns was set up on tripods. Nearby were a shipping pallet stacked with boxes of ammunition and a table full of AK-47s and sidearms, Glock 10 millimeters and some smaller stuff. I could also see a couple of cut-down pump guns, the kind with plated barrels and plastic stocks.

One wall was covered with nautical charts and highway maps. Dive tanks and wet suits littered the floor. Farther back stood a drafting table with a gooseneck lamp and a pile of blueprints and schematics. A portable welding rig had been shoved into one corner.

In the middle of the room was something big draped with an oversize Cuban flag.

Fontana sat down in an old armchair and cleared his throat.

"So. The plan is to hijack the *Norwegian Empress* and make it look like terrorism. That's the cover story. What's really going on is old-fashioned piracy. With your help, Matthew, we're going to whack a modern-day galleon."

"Yo-ho-ho and a bottle of rum!" Bryant piped up. He seemed to have quit worrying about me wearing a wire. Mellow now.

"I'm sure that in your role of security director for a big cruise line you've given some thought to this already," Fontana said. "Your *Empress* is a very vulnerable lady, the oldest and smallest member of the Festival fleet. Twelve hundred passengers and crew chugging along through the wild blue yonder with exactly three firearms on board. One locked up in the wheelhouse, one in the captain's quarters, and one under the chief mate's jacket. The galleons had cannons and armed escorts.

"I'm sure you've also run the numbers and figured out what's kept something like this from happening. The money just isn't there. If you took the drop box from the casino, the petty cash from the purser's office, and the play money out of every passenger's wallet, it wouldn't amount to a hundred grand. You guys even stopped carrying crew payroll, what, two years ago?"

I looked over at Manny. He was sitting on a piano bench picking his nose with his pinky and working on a crossword puzzle.

"Let me shift gears for a minute," Fontana said, getting up from the armchair and starting to pace. "Manuel, you feel free to pipe up. Back in the cowboy days, by which I mean the late seventies and early eighties in Miami, it was pretty simple for the cartels to launder the cash they were taking off the street. They just had their people walk into any bank on Brickell Avenue with a suitcase full of green and write a deposit slip. Then they would wire it offshore. In hindsight it seems incredible, but this went on for years. One day banks had to start reporting any cash deposits over ten thousand dollars, and all of a sudden moving the money became a monumental pain in the ass.

"At the same time the local DEA, meaning me and Kirk Semple and Gaspar González and some other underpaid overachievers, were setting up bogus brokerage houses and mortgage companies and seizing a lot of the swag, sending a message. Nowadays everyone's heard

about how hard it's supposedly gotten to smuggle cocaine into South Florida. But the flip side of the business
is equally tough. What good is selling a kilo of coke if
you can't get the revenue back to Bogotá? The proceeds
are harder to move than the product. If it's street money,
it's going to be in fives and tens and twenties, maybe
three times bulkier than powder. Every other week
some pathetic mule gets caught at the airport with fifty
thousand in cash stuck down his pants. The public
doesn't really get it.

"It's a big, fat cash-flow problem," he said. "It's a
problem that hasn't been solved, and maybe it never will
be. If you split up the money and carry it by courier, you
involve that many more people, it takes longer, you lose
a slice, and you generally have to pay more for delivery.
If you put the eggs in one basket and fly it out by prop
plane, you cut your costs but increase the risk. You could
lose all those eggs."

I was beginning to see where this was going.

"The *Empress* has made five trips from Miami to Havana since Congress relaxed the travel ban two months
ago. Each time she leaves port there's a big protest
by local Cubans, with lots of screaming and mega-
phones. And each time — this is the important part,
Matthew — each time, she's been secretly hauling raw
currency, a little more every trip. There are seven people

on earth who think they're the only ones who know about this. Or make that six. The guy who clued me in was lying on his back in a shower stall where some lifer mongoloid named Credence Breedlove shivved him through the liver over a piece of cornbread."

Fontana stopped pacing and turned toward me, taking off his jacket and rolling up his sleeves.

"The money stays on board in Havana and gets offloaded in Grand Cayman. They've got a warehouse about the size of this one a mile from the port. They repackage it and take it straight to the Bank of the Netherlands. It's gone like clockwork, so far. It's worked so well that next time around, the fat cats in Cali are upping the ante. A lot."

I looked around the room. It smelled like cement dust. I knew it was going to be Manny who answered my first question, and no one was going to say another word until I asked it, so I went ahead.

"How much?"

"Thirty million dollars," Manny said. "Approximately three and one-half tons."

They were waiting for some reaction, and it was hard not to give it to them.

"They don't even sort the shit till it gets to the islands," Bryant snorted. "They just run it through trash compactors and shrink-wrap it in polyurethane. Sloppiest motherfuckers I ever saw. Last time it was packed in tomato-sauce boxes."

"The inside man is Menoyo, the galley manager," Fontana said, reading my thoughts. "And your assistant security director, Neal Atlee."

I was feeling hot. I sat down on a stool.

"Say something, Matthew," Fontana said.

"This has been very entertaining. You want me to say something? Here's what I've got to say. It'll never work. And I'm not interested. And right now I'm going to start thinking how to get out of the position you've put me in by telling me this shit. I think what I'm going to do is pretend I fell asleep in a cab on the way to the Delano and had a bad dream, because that's what this is."

Something on the wall had been catching my eye for the last few minutes. I walked over and looked. It was a statement from Barnett Bank with my name on it. Credit reports listing charge-card accounts were pasted all over the cinder blocks.

"I'm surprised to hear you say you're not interested," Fontana said. "To be painfully blunt, Matthew, I think you could use a turnaround play in your life right now. You have two hundred thirty dollars in your checking account. You have an early retirement pension at GS-fourteen that pays you twenty-nine hundred a month gross. You have nine credit cards with a total balance up over eighty thousand dollars. And you have another three hundred twelve thousand to pay on your wife's medical bills. My condolences, incidentally."

He paused, and I watched something flicker across his face.

"You're forty-nine years old and living in a glorified flophouse. Something you may not know is that you're going to get fired in about three weeks. Tanel's bringing in Paul Lewis at twice your salary. One thing Tanel likes about him is he doesn't drink more than eight or ten shots of bourbon on any given weeknight. He even has a driver's license."

I turned around and looked at them. Kip was grinning. Krystal had put down her needlepoint and was working on her fingers with a nail file, humming to herself. Bryant was practicing his glare on Manny.

Fontana said, "Your contention that the plan won't work, I'm going to interpret that as meaning you have lots of questions about logistics. We can talk about that. But when all's said and done, this plan will work for the same reason smuggling millions of dollars in currency on a cruise ship works in the first place. It's never been done. No one expects it."

"Right," I said. "I'll play along. Let's say you manage to board a ship that's doing eighteen knots in the Gulf

Stream and somehow get control of twelve hundred passengers and crew. And sever communications. That's the plan, right?"

"Correct. More or less."

"What happens when someone hiding in a bathroom calls the Coast Guard on a cell phone?"

"Cell phones don't work twenty miles out at sea. And it doesn't matter, anyway. I seem to remember that you and I spent five tedious years on FBI reactive squads in Dallas before I had the good sense to switch over to DEA and you moved up to counterintelligence. Remember the bank robbers who didn't get caught? Fat Boy Frank? The Midnight Rambler? They were the ones who wore watches. Get in and get out."

"Matt?" Kip chimed in. "I took over a whole city in Angola one time with twelve guys and a tank, OK? Trust me, this is a can o' corn."

"Let's say you manage to off-load three tons of cash, presumably without anyone seeing you do it," I said. "Where are you going to run? You'll have forty-five minutes before the cavalry shows up, if that."

"You're probably right," Fontana said brightly. "The likelihood of getting detained is figured into the deal. We just don't plan on having anything in our possession that ties us to either the hijacking or the heist."

Kip had moved to the middle of the room. His hands were shaking again. It was something neurological — too much coke or steroids at some point in the past.

"You may not know this, but the first piece of mail you get in prison is a form letter from your State Farm rep canceling your life-insurance policy," Fontana said. "When I got done pouting, I decided to cook up a new insurance plan of my very own. You've been hearing the basic outline. Now let's look at some of the fine print. Go ahead, Kip."

Kip whipped the red-and-blue flag away, and I saw what was underneath. It was a garbage Dumpster, with some big white tubes fastened to the side.

"The war wagon!" Kip yelped.

The rim of the Dumpster was lined with thick rubber, a pressure seal. A box was welded to the lid with a dial, black wires coming off it.

"Positive buoyancy," Kip said, chucking me on the arm. He meant the white PVC pipes stuck on the sides. "You fill it up with moolah, and it still floats. But when you put a little weight to her, an anchor, she sinks. I tested it with bundles of newspapers. The anchor goes on a cable that clips in here." He bent down and swung the container around, pointing out a ring on the back. The Dumpster was on casters. "You set the timer. When the timer goes off, it releases the anchor cable, and the

whole enchilada floats to the surface. This is just the pro-
totype. The one we're going to use has a radio tracker on
it, so we can grab it fast once it pops up."

"Tell him how deep it is," Bryant said. "That's what
blows my mind."

"That part of the Stream, you're talking almost a
thousand meters," Kip said.

"I like to think about all that money sitting down
there under the ocean," added Bryant. "In the dark,
man. Sittin' down there just waiting. Whales and shit
swimming by."

"Hey, Matthew," Fontana said. "All those years you
were chasing spies and kidnappers and white-collar
bullshit artists. Didn't you ever want to show 'em how
it's really done?"

6

IT WAS AFTER MIDNIGHT when I got home. I locked the door and cranked open the louvered windows, and for a time I stood in the darkness naked to the waist, letting the cool breeze from the beach play over my skin.

I left the lights off and thought about taking a shower, and while I thought about it, I lay on the couch and tried to stop thinking. I couldn't, though. I wondered about Neal Atlee, how long had he been dirty; whether Hector was involved; and was there anyone else on the inside. Did Fontana turn them, or had they been working for someone else before him? This was all beside the point, I decided.

I closed my eyes. Seeing Kip had stirred up a lot of things I didn't want to stir up. I dozed off, and below me were rice paddies and jungles full of orange fire. I saw some of the Montagnards in a village up north. Then things got worse. A guy was getting pushed out of a chopper with his hands tied behind his back. For a while I was falling too. Then I got up and went into the bathroom and flicked on the light, and when I lifted the lid of the toilet, it was my wife's face looking up at me, her whole head there in the toilet. Her hair had fallen out from the chemotherapy, all but a few wisps, and she wore bright lipstick, a shocking scarlet against her porcelain skin. She opened her eyes very slowly and started to smile, and her eyes were made of emeralds. Then the window blinds clattered against the wall, and I woke up and decided I wasn't going back to sleep for a while.

I put on some shorts and a sweatshirt and went for a walk, over to Meridian, then up Meridian to Fifth. I cut across to Washington and bought a bottle of bourbon at the market halfway up the block and considered having a pull right there on the street. Thursday night was for locals, and couples and groups of kids were leaving clubs and going to others. Walking north along Washington, I saw one young guy up against a wall taking a leak right out in the open. His girlfriend was laughing, and then she fell down on the sidewalk, but by the time I went over to help her, she was back on her feet, laughing again, leaning against a car. Muscle boys were comparing notes outside the Warsaw Ballroom, having come out to catch some air. At Fourteenth I crossed over to Ocean and turned south again, sticking to the beach side of the street, where I could see all the cafés and neon but not be too close.

I walked right past the Cardozo and almost didn't see her sitting alone at a deuce, watching me. I crossed the street and stood on the sidewalk. The tables were about three feet up from street level.

"You keep late hours," she said.

"I was just going out for a jog."

She smiled. "That must be your bottle of Gatorade, then."

She meant the bourbon in the paper bag. I had forgotten about that.

"I decided I didn't feel like jogging."

She was wearing a T-shirt and jeans. I thought she looked even better without any makeup. Different, anyway.

"Where's the sugar baron?"

"He passed out about an hour ago," she answered. "Back at the Delano."

"So your shift is over."

"Very good."

"He's staying there, and you're staying here?"

She nodded. "This place is more my speed, and it's a lot cheaper."

I was about to say it would be even cheaper than that to just spend the night with the guy, but maybe he snored or something.

"He's going out to L.A. with Tim in the morning," she added. "I'm supposed to wake him up at nine and put him on a plane. Tim's trying to dazzle him into producing a movie."

"You're not going?"

"I don't fly."

Some tourists came down the steps to get in a taxi, and I had to move to the side.

"You're welcome to join me for a drink," she offered. "I think I'd like to know who you are exactly."

So I introduced myself and sat down at the table. Julia Bonnell was who I was sitting with.

"Are you a cop, Matthew?"

"I run the security department for a cruise line."

"So you're an ex-cop."

"I'm an ex–FBI agent. I retired three years ago."

"You look pretty young to be retired from anything. Didn't you like it?"

"I liked parts of it. Toward the end I became a supervisor, which was probably a mistake. It got to be like an office job."

"I see you're missing an important digit."

She was looking at my right hand resting on the table, the stump of the index finger. I put my hand in my lap. "A bad afternoon with a garbage disposal."

"Show me," she said.

I reached across the table. She took my thumb in one hand and held my fingers in the other, narrowing her eyes.

"An intern did this on a busy night. You can see here where he didn't pull the flap quite tight enough as he was sewing it up."

When she turned my hand over, I smiled.

"What?"

"I've never had my palm read," I said.

"I see long life and good fortune. And healing problems."

"The bone got infected."

She let go and leaned back in her chair. "Try an alligator bite next time."

"An alligator bite?"

"Garbage disposals don't leave clean shear marks. You need to work on your fibbing."

The waiter came by, and Julia ordered a drink.

"If you don't mind my asking, what were you doing at the Delano earlier tonight?" she asked.

"I was supposed to meet a friend at the bar. He never showed up."

"He?"

"Yeah. Another retired agent. We used to work together. He wanted some feedback on an investment we've been looking at." This was mostly true, I figured.

She thought about that. Then she smiled. "You're sweet."

"I am?"

"I just figured it out. You don't have any money with you."

"I've got about a dollar and forty cents."

"You want a drink, but you wouldn't be caught dead letting a woman pick up the tab."

"A considerably younger woman."

"You've been sitting there thinking how you'd like to pour yourself a nice big slug out of that bottle, haven't you?"

"The management would frown."

I couldn't get her in focus. She seemed very direct, but it felt like was she was coming around corners from odd directions.

"Let's go upstairs and I'll get us some ice and glasses," she suggested. "That way you can be the one who's buying. How does that sound?"

"Are you sure you want to do that?"

"Why not?"

"You hardly know me. It's late."

"This is how people get to know each other. I'm just inviting you up to my room for a drink."

Not defensive, just saying it like it was.

• • •

WHATEVER I IMAGINED was going to happen, it turned out to be something different. When we got to Julia's room, I had a sense of how they built things in the fifties, which is to say, small: two double beds, a kitchenette through one door. The thing that caught my eye was a big brown case in one corner near a set of doors that led to a narrow balcony. It was a case for some kind of musical instrument, with a handle on the side and three metal clasps. Across the room I noticed a stethoscope hanging from a hook on the door.

Julia went to get ice while I looked around and found a pair of those brittle plastic cups they put in hotel bathrooms, all covered with saran wrap. When she came back, I poured the drinks.

She took a cello out of the big case and started to play. After about two minutes someone pounded on the floor upstairs, and she opened her eyes and stopped.

"I guess it *is* late," she said.

"I liked that. What was it?"

"Part of a sonata. It's by a Hungarian guy named Zoltán Kodály."

We went out onto the balcony. Two miles offshore we could see where all the ships were anchored while the channel was getting cleared.

"It seems like there's a lot of boats out there doing nothing," she said.

"The port closed down for a couple days. They're just waiting until it opens again."

She nodded. "I heard something about that. There was an explosion."

"Yes."

She took a sip from her glass. "Bourbon has gotten fashionable. My father used to drink Maker's Mark back when it was just whiskey. He was from Tennessee."

"Yeah? My dad was from Kentucky. A coal miner, he and his brothers. They all drank Jim Beam."

"Southern gentlemen," she said, and we clicked our glasses together.

"You said 'used to.'"

"He died when I was nineteen," she said. "He was a music teacher. That's what concert pianists become when they don't quite make it as concert pianists. He and his wife adopted me."

"Well, you've followed in his footsteps. With the music, I mean."

"I try to be a pragmatist, Matt. The music is just for fun. How long were you married?"

"How do you know I was?"

She laughed. "Lots of reasons. One is you've been wearing a wedding band until just recently. There's still a circle of white skin around your ring finger."

I held up my hand and saw she was right. "We got married right after college. She died two years ago."

"Kids?"

"No."

"No?"

"When the time came, she wasn't able to. And I didn't want any. So it worked out."

"Did it?"

"Well, it worked out how it worked out."

She didn't say anything for a time. Then she sounded angry.

"You think she was a saint, don't you, Matt?"

"She was a good person. I couldn't find much fault with her."

"Maybe you stopped looking very hard."

"It was a quiet marriage."

"What does that mean, 'a quiet marriage'? Was she happy?"

"Toward the end? Of course not. She was dying of cancer."

"Not toward the end. At all."

I didn't answer. I wondered why we were talking about any of this.

"So no kids, huh?"

I looked at her. She had her back up against the balcony railing, watching me. And now *I* was angry. Who was she to ask about my wife, what we had had together? Who was anyone to ask about that?

And more to the point, maybe: what the hell was I doing here, on this balcony where I had no business being? Trying to get laid? Christ, what a joke. I hadn't been on a date in twenty-five years, and I wasn't particularly good at it then. As for sex, I could barely remember what it was like. Or not sex; fucking wasn't what I had begun to forget. You couldn't: it catcalled and smirked and beat a dinner gong from the cover of every magazine; it cut farts and lit them on fire and shot itself out of a cannon on all five hundred channels of every TV set nowadays. No, I mean the edges of it, not the outright act; what it's like to hold someone. The ache of that and the sheer weirdness of it, the terrible nakedness you feel skin to skin with someone you care about. The mystery parts.

"She got pregnant our first year together, before we

were married," I said, surprised I was saying it. "It was bad timing. Money was tight. I'm not sure we knew we were going to stay together at that point, anyway. She wouldn't have an abortion, even if we could have found a way to do that. You have to understand how different it was then."

"So?"

"So we decided — she agreed to give up the child. I told her there would be plenty of time later for kids, but it didn't work out that way. It was a girl. It could have been you." I looked at her and wished it was.

She went inside, and I looked over my shoulder as she walked toward the kitchenette, watching the way she moved in her jeans, no bra, the T-shirt pulling tight.

"Do you want some coke?" she asked.

I was going to explain that soft drinks hurt my teeth, but she was in the kitchen doorway holding a Baggie with a half inch of white powder. She sat down at a desk against the wall and cut out four lines and went to work on one without waiting for my answer.

"I didn't really expect to see you again," she said. "Or at least not so soon. I wasn't very discreet the first time, was I?"

"I'm not complaining."

She rolled her eyes and then stood up and offered me the chair and a length of soda straw. I shook my head.

"The sugar baron is beginning to bore me," she said. "Not beginning, in fact. So I'm looking for the next gig. That's not an advertisement, I'm just trying to explain how I'm a little crazy lately. This is awkward, isn't it? I normally keep my socializing separate from my work."

"When's this gig up?"

"Tomorrow. I'm going to take a few weeks off. I'd like to go someplace where there's snow."

She seemed content to stand there, sipping the bourbon and looking at me, swaying slightly, like she could still hear the echo of music.

"You don't know what you're missing," she said, glancing at the table, giving an exaggerated sniff.

"What about after your vacation?"

She shrugged. "I have a couple of offers."

She was looking at me carefully now, her gray eyes sparkling.

"At the Delano, we were having drinks at the inside bar, and I saw you get on the elevator. You went to the fifteenth floor."

I didn't say anything.

"Later on you came back down with some people, including a certain Jack Fontana."

"That's where your next gig is coming from?"

"I like to know a little bit about who I'm dealing with. Before I deal with them."

"What's he offering?"

"Union scale." She smiled. "He mentioned a real-estate project that's about to pay off. So?"

"Fontana's OK," I said. "We mostly knew each other years ago. I'm not sure where his head's at these days."

She kept looking at me, her pupils seeming even darker, the irises full of light. I wanted to touch her.

"Where did you meet him?" she asked.

I thought about that. It would have been when we were boys, eight or nine, at a crossroads town called Etna Furnace.

"He's my brother," I told her. "My stepbrother."

She had been on her way to taking another sip from her drink, but the glass stopped in midair. "Oh, shit," she said.

"Yeah."

At the door I took her hand. As she was letting go, she ran her fingers along my wrist in a way that was better than any kiss.

"See you around, Matthew Shannon," she said. "Let me know how that investment turns out. Yours and Jack's."

I walked down the hall; then I went back and knocked. She opened the door and laughed when she heard what I wanted.

She went inside the room and came back, handing me the whole Baggie.

• • •

ON THE WAY DOWN in the elevator I had a bump, then another for good measure. She had set me thinking. On the street outside I walked and thought about things and kept coming back to my wife, how we had lived together, why it seemed so important. The mornings, for instance, something as simple as that. I had liked the mornings best, the hour we had together before we went to work, waking up and getting in each other's way in the bathroom or getting dressed, that private lack of privacy. We were always together that way, whenever we weren't working, and our off-hours weren't about lounging on the couch with our clothes off. We did things; we got things done; it was a partnership. She was better at certain things, and I was better at others, and some of those things were backward from what you might expect. I liked washing dishes, for example, and didn't particularly mind vacuuming floors. Vacuuming reminded me of plowing; so I would vacuum away and pretend I was a giant, plowing. On the other hand, I didn't enjoy cooking things on a grill; I could never get it quite right, so she did that. And lots of other things. When I had to practice at the firing range, she would go with me. She was amazing with a shotgun, a lot better than me; she was better than I was the first time she picked one up.

How would I explain that to Julia Bonnell, even if I wanted to? And if you didn't explain the whole thing, every part, why get into it at all? I sat down on a bench and let my mind run.

She liked flowers. It sounds hokey, but she did, and I mean really liked them. She knew all their names, and that wasn't any easy trick because Miami's full of oddball plants — bromeliads, for example, as big and bright as the birds out in the Everglades. She wasn't as good with the birds — spoonbills, purple gallinules, night herons — but damn near.

When you work for the Bureau, you start early, seven a.m., and work late. The mornings are like a contest, especially with the younger guys. Younger gals, too, I should say, because by the time I retired there were quite a few of those, which at first seemed strange but later I thought was a good thing. You get together in the squad room, go over the duty roster and get ready for the day, check weapons and drink coffee and shoot the bull, the young ones all acting bold and pretending they didn't wish they were still home in bed instead of wearing a suit and a gun. Toward the end, I was in charge of some of them, and after a long weekend I would ask them how they had spent it. One of them might have a boat, and they'd all be out on Biscayne Bay, fishing, or at the clubs up in Lauderdale, drinking, chasing tail. Very occasionally one of them, maybe looking to score some points, would ask me what *I'd* done. And they would try not to laugh when I told them. Yes, I took my wife to Fairchild Tropical Garden. What, and looked at flowers? That's right. Trees, too, all kinds. The guy who started the place, some rich cat, he collected them from all over the world. A part of the garden even had cactuses, which I couldn't believe the first time I saw them because it rains every day in Miami in the summer. But there they were.

How could you explain that? Or the zoo? We went to the zoo all the time. I damn sure wasn't going to tell anyone in the squad room about that, but we did go, and we both liked it, although neither of us was too keen on reptiles. At night, in bed, we would play a game, pretending to be different animals. We would make all sorts of sounds, cracking each other up, until things got serious, and we sort of shifted into the old human sounds, the human-animal sounds that go along with all that.

She had been really shy. For the first couple of years we were together, she would wait until I turned the lights off before she got undressed and slipped into bed. But she liked everything between us, I could tell by the sounds she made; softly and sometimes not so softly at all. There's no faking that.

And here's the thing: sometimes, after she fell asleep, I would close the bathroom door and look in the mirror and ask myself what there was to love in *that?* I was sure no movie star. My shoulders were thick and narrow. My hair was a sandy color that was no color at all, nothing anyone would remember, and always too thin to stay in place very long after I combed it; and my eyes were the color of mud puddles. I had, it seemed to me, too much in the way of fur on my chest, and my legs were bony, the one polka-dotted with shrapnel scars. I mean, why would a woman like any of that? But she seemed to. No, she did. And she had been the homecoming queen of Frostproof High; she was beautiful.

She wasn't one of these touchy-feely people, but at odd times, out of the blue, when we would be walking together, I would be surprised to feel her take my hand. It was like what happened on a lot of mornings: she would put both her arms around my shoulders and look into my eyes, not saying anything; or some mornings just lay her head against my neck and stand there in the kitchen. Not every day, but more mornings than not. I would wait for it. I came to live for that, secretly, a part of me waiting for it to stop happening, but it never did. I played a game with myself, counting the days before it would happen again. Sometimes there would be three or four or five even, but never a week — never. It was just something she did for her own reasons, and I never asked her about it.

She had never seen snow or been on a ship. She hadn't been around as much as I had, but she sure had read a lot more. I liked to read too, even if I didn't see the point in fiction. To judge from the number of bookstores, we were the only two bookworms in Miami, at least when we first moved here. There was one store, though, Books & Books, that a guy had started, and he hung in there. We went to it a lot, and we both loved it.

Once in a while we'd decide to watch TV — we owned one mainly so people wouldn't think we were strange — and she would bring me her hairbrush. I would sit on the couch, and she would sit on the floor between my legs, and I would brush her hair. I was terrible at it at first, but I got better after I realized she wasn't so delicate as all that, and it was OK to pull on her hair, at least some. Her hair was a whole world. I dreamed about it all the time.

How could I explain that to someone like Julia Bonnell? Or to someone even younger, say the club kids I had seen on the street when I walked here, the ravers and body-piercers? They swam in a different sea. Maybe we all did; six billion souls, six billion seas.

Which one did I swim in now? With her gone, nothing was left between me and the conclusions I'd drawn that I wished I hadn't. I remembered a map of the moon I had seen, with the name of the biggest crater spelled out in letters so official looking you almost missed the joke: the Sea of Fertility. I thought I understood the guy behind the telescope somewhere who'd named it that.

It was not like anything I had ever experienced, and I thought I'd lived quite a bit even before I got married. But living with her was something completely different, and it kept getting better. For me, anyway. For her, too, I had believed, right up until a couple of years before the end. Then I would see something in her eyes, like the shadow a jet casts crossing the sun on a sunny day, startling and then gone. I was pretty sure I knew what it was.

● ● ●

Fontana thought he had my number, but he was way off target. I lay in my own bed later that night and tried to remember what he had said the other day, something about going your whole life not knowing if you're a coward. My experience was, it just didn't come up. It was something people in movies thought about. Maybe he was saying that it ought to come up, that everything was watered down nowadays. It didn't matter. That didn't matter, and neither did some credit-card bills. Getting fired was a bit more of a problem. So was a black box the size of a cigarette pack with my fingerprints all over it. But even that seemed a long way off, music in another room.

I looked at the ceiling, the shadows there. The more I thought about it, the more I knew what the real problem was and didn't want to face it. It was so stupid, so much smaller than I wanted it to be: I was bored. Bored, and I couldn't remember the last time I hadn't been. I could leave, just get some things in a bag and drive away, go north, then west. Yes, it was unrealistic. But at this point, what was realistic?

After a while light started coming through the blinds. I got up and waited in the street until a cab came along, then rode across the causeway into downtown Miami and found a pay phone in the lobby of the Everglades Hotel.

Fontana answered after five rings. I heard a woman's voice in the background sounding sleepy and pissed off.

"You know who this is?"

"It's a little early, Matt."

"Why don't we get together sometime next week?"

There was a long pause. "Next week is too late. As in after the fact."

"You're kidding."

"Nope."

I took a deep breath. "Tomorrow?"

"You mean today, right?"

"I guess so."

"Where?"

"The Cardozo. One o'clock?"

"That's fine. Please tell me you're not calling me from your apartment."

"No. My phone's cut off."

He laughed. "Of course it is."

I had asked the cabbie to wait, but he didn't. I went out on Biscayne Boulevard and walked until I found a Haitian guy asleep in the backseat of a yellow station wagon. I rousted him, and he yawned and got in the front and started driving.

When we hit the on-ramp to the causeway, I put the straw down in the Baggie and worked on it slow and easy. Pretty soon I had a nice, icy hum starting up in my sinuses. I caught the driver glancing in the rearview mirror. There was a moment when we held each other's gaze, not saying anything. He had the radio locked on a station that was giving the news in Creole.

"You want some, you can have it," I said.

After about five seconds he started slowing down, putting on his turn blinker.

The sun was coming up between the new high-rises on South Beach, throwing light on Government Cut. I was thinking maybe I would have the guy drop me next to Penrod's, walk down on the beach and look at the water, maybe even go swimming.

Jesus, I thought, this is it. Fucking Fontana, back at it again.

PART TWO

WATER

7

The tourists were milling around on Mallory Pier, drinking rumrunners and watching the trained cats jump through flaming hoops, the guy who could juggle chain saws and get out of straitjackets, everyone waiting to see the sunset. It was going to be a disappointment because a big cloud bank reached all the way across the sky off Key West.

Three days had passed since the freighter blew up and sank in the Miami ship channel, and now we were four hours south of there, sitting in deck chairs on the back of Fontana's cabin cruiser, the *Ya-Ya,* at anchor in the lee of Christmas Tree Island. Fontana leaned forward to study the newsletter the cabin stewards slipped under the stateroom doors aboard the *Norwegian Empress.* The

Empress herself lay a mile to the south, across Key West Harbor and just beyond the tourists, tied up in her berth behind the Truman Annex.

"It's like something out of *The Twilight Zone,*" Bryant said, talking about the floor show on the cruise ship. "Old Broadway shit, they don't even sing the songs all the way through. There's this Bahamian guy who plays the steel drums from ten in the morning till suppertime and then guess what? He puts on a tux and does this tap routine. I wanted to cap his ass right there. I mean it was degrading, man."

"Fuck you, Kunta Kinte," Kip said. "It was fun. They had a comedian later on, you didn't even see him. Tomorrow night it's Max the Magician."

Krystal was on the bow with a Walkman, tanning her backside in a thong bikini. For ten minutes Kip had been sitting on the gunwale wearing a rubber monster mask, the Creature from the Black Lagoon. The mask, the way Kip kept lifting it up and blowing his nose one nostril at a time over the side of the boat, it was starting to get to me.

"You expect me to work with this retard?" Bryant now, giving Kip the glare, talking to Fontana.

Fontana kept looking at the newsletter. "How many people in the casino?"

"It's not a gambling crowd," Bryant said. He folded

his arms across his chest. "About eighty at any one time. The dealers couldn't get jobs mopping floors in Vegas. There's one guy was in there at the blackjack table counting cards all night, they just kept comping him drinks."

Kip said, "Three hundred in the Neptune Lounge watching the shows. Another sixty in the bars. Everyone else crashes by eleven."

"How many skeet guns?" I asked just to see if they'd paid attention.

"Six, Mr. Security Chief." Kip pulled a yellow shotgun cartridge out of the pocket of his shorts and threw it at Bryant's head. It missed and bounced off the cabin doorway. "Twenty-gauge Remingtons with bird shot. The purser locks 'em up in a deck box around five thirty with all the ammo. You should see this one fat guy. He shoots from the hip and nails those birds every freakin' time. He's some kind of retired doctor from Kansas."

"That's impressive to you, isn't it?" Bryant said, bending down to pick up the shotgun cartridge. "I guess when you grow up in a trailer eating possum stew and Moon-Pies, that sort of thing is a big thrill, right? A fat man on a cruise ship who's adept at shooting clay pigeons?"

"Yeah," said Kip. "It's sort of like, for you, getting fucked up the ass by a big Cuban prison guard. I wish I could've seen the look on your Black Panther face getting off that Seven Forty-Seven in Havana. Did you think ol' Fidel was going to give you a cigar, maybe have you make a speech or something? You and your Afro?"

I wondered why Fontana wasn't saying anything. What was strange, I got the feeling Bryant and Kip were getting along just fine. Bryant: never caught, never locked up since his stint in a Cuban jail in the late seventies; a Marxist hothead and onetime airline hijacker turned top-notch armored-car heister. I knew exactly one thing about armored cars, the only thing worth knowing: there's absolutely no way to jack one without being prepared to kill somebody; no bluffing, no hesitation. From what Fontana said, Bryant had antifreeze for blood, and three murder warrants on him in three different states. Kip: a stone killer with more trigger time under his belt than a Ranger platoon; I doubted his diastolic blood pressure hit ninety even when he was pulling out someone's windpipe in a Central American shithole fifty miles from anywhere with plumbing.

Bryant threw the cartridge in the water. "You have no idea what you're talking about," he said. "This mercenary rep we've all heard about, you ever fight for something you believe in? You got any beliefs at all? I'd like to hear one actual idea you ever had. Go ahead."

"OK," said Kip, adjusting his mask. "Topless mermaids."

"That's your idea, huh?"

"That's it."

"You want to expand on that, make yourself intelligible?"

"Krystal used to work at Weeki Wachee Spring," Kip said. "Our plan is to start a mermaid show down here, but with more skin. We're thinking of South Beach, maybe have some mermen jump in the tank with the girls, bring in the butt-pirate crowd."

"You going to let my homies look at your mermaids? You got any bootylicious sisters lined up to do some swimmin'? I bet you don't."

"You're right, we don't. And to answer your first question, anyone will be welcome at Wet Dreams, irregardless of their racial persuasion. Coons included. Just not ex-Commie hijacker coons."

We had been out to Stock Island the night before to look at Kip's lobster boat. The Dumpster was chained to the deck and covered with a plastic tarp. We stood around and smoked cigarettes, and that was that. At seven thirty this morning, Saturday, Fontana and I had met the *Empress* as she worked her bow and stern thrusters and settled into her berth behind the Truman

Annex and began off-loading old ladies and honey-mooners with fresh sunburns. Bryant had come down the gangway in his Dirty Harry Ray-Bans, followed by Kip and Krystal in Panama hats and matching Hawaiian shirts. As we were walking down a side street, Fontana passed out and fell on a café table where a pair of twinks were having Bloody Marys. He was out for only a minute, and when he came to, he said it was some medication he was taking. The twinks looked like they'd been up all night and didn't mind people passing out on their table, like it happened all the time.

Before the *Empress* left Miami on Friday afternoon, I had gone on board and put a paper sack with a pair of SIG-Sauers and flash suppressors inside one of the fire-hose cabinets on the promenade deck. Kip and Bryant and Krystal checked on the guns while they rode the ship from Miami down to Key West. There was nothing more to say without repeating ourselves, but that's not the way Fontana saw it. He kept asking about the lay-out, where people spent the most time. Except for plant-ing the pistols, I hadn't done anything. We were just hanging out in Key West for the weekend, fishing bud-dies on a fishing boat.

I was learning things about my fishing buddies. Manny had hooked up with Krystal years ago to take down traveling diamond merchants in lonely hotel rooms across the Midwest. The only pull he'd done lasted three years because he wouldn't roll on her, and I could understand why. When she was still a high-school cheerleader and aspiring cosmetologist, Krystal had spent one summer vacation tracking down her own rapists, a pair of Outlaw bikers from Winnipeg. When she found them, she served them a special dinner: their own balls, in a homemade marinara sauce.

How it stood: the *Empress* would stay to let everyone get drunk on Duval Street and go see Ernest Hemingway's house and Mel Fisher's Treasure Museum, then it would leave for Havana tonight, which happened to be Halloween.

"I remember back in the seventies you could go down there and roll a doob and *really* watch the sunset," Fontana said, looking across the harbor at the crowd on the pier. "I'm surprised no one's started charging admission."

"They have," I said. "Some crackhead got arrested last week for selling tickets. It was in the paper."

No one said anything, so I added, "Back in the seventies they didn't have the guy with the house cats. This French guy. He's got a whip like a lion tamer."

"You can't make a cat do shit," Bryant said.

"That's what I thought, but he does. He has to keep running over and popping them on the head with his knuckle. One of 'em docs flips. There's another one that walks a tightrope."

"The thing about cats I always wondered," said Fontana, "they've got this fur coat that covers their whole body, so how did God know exactly where to cut holes for the eyes?"

Bryant stopped digging in the ice chest. "I wish you wouldn't say things like that. It makes you sound imbalanced." He was looking around for a bottle opener until he realized the beer in his hand was a twist-off.

"Tell me about the engine room," said Fontana, back again. He shook a couple of Percocets out of a prescription bottle just as the sun slipped under the cloud bank and disappeared below the horizon. The tourists clapped.

8

WHILE WE SAT around on the *Ya-Ya,* Manny was anchored on the edge of the Marquesas, thirty miles from Key West. He was out there alone in Kip's lobster boat thinking up a seven-letter word for "noted Bolshevik," working on one of his crossword puzzles; that, or he was long gone, getting on a plane bound for New York, Bogotá, anywhere. Fontana didn't seem worried, though. He had something heavy on the guy, something to really make him jump.

Manny ran a car dealership in Coral Gables, used Mercedes and Jags, other high-end stuff. In between being an accountant and a diamond thief, he had run around the Keys in a lot of loaded-down speedboats, so he got stuck with lobster duty. The plan was to meet him in the Marquesas, anchor Fontana's cabin cruiser for a few hours, and head out from there in the lobster boat. Manny's job would be to stay with the *Ya-Ya* until we were ready for him to pick us up at sea.

It was time for Kip and Krystal and Bryant to get back on board the *Empress*. I watched Fontana get in the dinghy with them and head for Key West Bight, and then I lay down on one of the quarter berths in the salon and dozed. In a dream I saw my wife in moonlight, walking into the surf on Bimini. When she turned around and started back from the sea, something dark was behind her that seemed like a storm cloud at first but then came closer and moved like something alive. I was running down the beach as fast as I could run, but the dark thing drew her farther into the water. She was smiling even while it happened, and I was running in deep sand, screaming as she moved away from me into darkness. Then I was drowning, and then I was waking up.

I came to hearing a motor pass by. It was almost nine thirty. Fontana had been gone an hour and a half.

I sat up and put my feet on the teak cabin sole and tried to think. The thing for me to do was get out of here now while everything was still a joke. There was a water taxi that picked people up from boats and took them to shore, and in a minute I would hail it on the radio.

There was probably a number to call, but I didn't see my cell phone anywhere in the salon.

The town was starting to get wild. Outside, from the stern, I could hear two bands playing. Hundreds of people were on the pier across the harbor. Three guys were throwing a football around, until one of them missed a pass, and the football landed in the water.

I opened the cooler and grabbed a cold one and stood there remembering a night thirty years ago when Jack and I had gone over the mountains in our patched-together uniforms to play a school rich enough to have lights on its football field. The game was one we didn't have a prayer of winning. In my memory Jack stumbled backward, his thumb broken and one eye swollen shut from a lineman's cleat, and let loose a sixty-yard Hail Mary. The football had spiraled through electric night, and time slowed down and nearly stopped as my hands reached up to draw in the world and connect with him, against the odds. The clock ran dry and made us champions. And the next night: me and Jack tearing up Ironton with a pair of hardscrabble blondes, twin sisters from a hollow even farther out Coal Haul Road than our own, the whole town buying us drinks. In the last and roughest tavern, I had got up to take a leak and come back to an empty table. Jack was gone, along with the sisters, and later he would tell me about his big night in the backseat with both of them. Our father — Jack's father, my stepfather — sat on the porch steps and smoked his pipe the next morning while Jack and I beat each other bloody in the yard. The skirmish was an even draw, like always: I was bigger; Jack was that much meaner. And limping back from the creek, the two of us side by side but ten yards apart, I had to laugh, and I laughed now. It was just how he was. I'd accepted it long ago.

Fontana was the trickster, the jack-in-the-box, the carnival barker who slipped beneath a corner of the tent and doubled as the lion tamer. He was an undercover movie mogul whose cast and crew and audience were everyone he met on any given day. What brought us to Key West was just another episode for him, his latest act. But not for me. This wasn't a card trick or a football game or some dick-measuring contest for a pair of back-country blondes with straight razors in their purses. This was real.

In particular, the endgame bothered me. Fontana said he'd arranged for bail money, $50,000 apiece, with the idea that we would almost certainly get stopped and questioned after we hit the *Empress* and made a getaway. But what if that wasn't enough? What if things got complicated?

Fontana was going to get us killed. I was insane for being here. As soon as he got back, I would take the dinghy and head for shore.

That was it then. It was settled. What I'd been thinking two days ago was just late-night excitement, the coke doing the thinking for me. It was moon-madness, nothing more.

But I did owe him, that was the thing.

I got another beer and went inside. In the head I found some suntan lotion and untied the drawstring on my shorts. I closed my eyes so I didn't have to look in the mirror and tried to hold on an image of Krystal with her Walkman, asleep in sunlight. Just when I was going with it, I remembered how one of her legs was much thinner than the other, and pretty soon instead of Krystal, I was thinking of Julia Bonnell. I was seeing her at the Delano in the shadows by the pool, and at first I had the coolness of the air next to the pool and her there, just her smiling. But seeing her made me hear her, too. Words came with the images now, and I was losing it. I noticed that I couldn't bring back parts of how she looked, even though I had seen her two days ago. I was pretty sure I was never going to see her again.

I was hearing the sound of my cell phone going off, and then I was grabbing for a towel, pushing open the door of the little bathroom compartment. I found the phone behind the weatherfax and mashed the talk button.

I heard: "Bring me up to speed."

The phone slipped out of my hand and clattered onto the navigation table. I picked it up, wiping coconut oil off my hands.

"Matthew?"

It was Tanel's voice.

"Yes, I'm here."

"How have you spent the last two days? I'm told you haven't set foot in the office or kept anyone there apprised of your activities."

I exhaled slowly. "You asked me to run my own investigation. That's what I'm doing. It involves interviewing select subjects, some of them out of town. I'm in Key West right now."

A pause. "What conclusions have you drawn?"

"That the letter in the *Herald* was real. The freighter bombing was orchestrated by disaffected local Cubans."

"I would say that bodes well for Festival Cruise Lines, wouldn't you?"

"Yes. As I tried to indicate in our last meeting, I think the people behind the freighter bombing would think twice before targeting a cruise ship."

I heard the sound of a hand muffling the receiver; then Tanel came back on. "Take tomorrow off, Matthew."

"I generally do on Sunday."

"You're Catholic, aren't you?"

"That's right."

"Good for you. Listen, you need to pace yourself. You don't know how long your inquiry might last. And try to keep the cork in the bottle."

"Is there a particular reason —"

"Call me in Chicago on Monday."

The line went dead.

I leaned against the door of the toilet with my arms folded, trying to think, and finally gave up and shook my head and laughed.

There was half a loaf of bread beside a microwave in the galley. I found a plate in the cabinet and put some bread slices on it and opened the little refrigerator. I took jars of mustard and mayonnaise from the door shelf and found some sliced turkey and cheddar cheese.

When I had fixed the sandwich, I sat down at the nav station and switched on the lamp. I flipped through a Festival Cruise Lines brochure, looking at the pictures of young couples who were obviously models and old couples who were even more obviously models. There were lots of photos of the older ones sitting down to elegant suppers. One picture showed a washed-up movie star who was the company celebrity. He was hamming it up for the camera, holding his sunglasses in one hand and gesturing with the other toward some little cartoon maps of various cruise routes. The itinerary for the Eight-Day Western Caribbean Adventure had a star next to it to show that it was something new. Arrows starting in Miami went on to Key West and Havana, then over to Cozumel on the Yucatán Peninsula, in Mexico. From there the arrows kept going around the back side of Cuba to the Caymans and Jamaica, then through the Windward Passage and up the Bahama Channel to Miami again.

At the top of the page was a tiny silhouette of the *Norwegian Empress,* with specs listed underneath it. Gross tonnage, 22,000. Overall length, 524 feet. Beam, 78 feet. Draft, 18 feet. Cruising speed, 21 knots. Passengers, 900. Crew, 350. I knew the crew figures were exaggerated. Two hundred and fifty would be more accurate, working double shifts for months at a time for next to nothing, sending their wages back to Mindanao, Port-au-Prince, Mexico City, Manila. This time of year, the off-season, there were probably fewer than 700 paying customers, plus another 50 to 60 perk passages thrown in.

"Key West, Florida, is the scenic southernmost point in the continental United States," I read. *"Downtown, you'll*

*find great shopping and delicious island delights like the fa-
mous Key lime pie. A visit isn't complete without a peek at
the town's historic 19th century gingerbread mansions."*

I had set my plate down on top of a nautical chart, and
now I put the brochure aside and looked at the chart
while I finished the first half of the sandwich. Fontana
had penciled a line from Key West to Havana. Halfway
along the line he had made a small, strong X and written
latitude and longitude coordinates off to the side.

Another X and another set of coordinates were over
on the right, along the southern edge of the Marquesas.
A shorter, dotted line connected the two X's, and a compass heading was written above it. The Marquesas were
tiny gray spots floating in a cloud of pale blue, but south
and east of there the color bled away into white, where
the water dropped below thirty fathoms. It was all white
along the route the *Empress* would take, nothing but
deep water.

There were various symbols and notations on the
chart I didn't understand. I decided that the sandwich
needed a lettuce leaf, so I went back to the galley and
pulled open the refrigerator door. I couldn't find any lettuce, but something else was inside the crisper drawer.

Blood.

I pulled out two units and read the labels; they were
both A-positive. Six bags total, from a blood bank in

Hialeah, and all the expiration dates read tomorrow. I opened the other drawer, and it was full of liter bags of IV fluid: three clear, two tinged green. There were some smaller bags, one of them labeled with the name of an antibiotic, another that said *Fluorouracil*.

I knelt down and pulled everything out of the drawer. At the bottom were three hard-plastic boxes, each with ten glass vials. The black block letters on the side of each vial read *morphine sulfate*. I put everything back in the drawer and closed it and ate the rest of the sandwich standing there in the galley.

Suddenly I wasn't sure of anything, not anything at all. Or maybe one thing: the reason Fontana had popped up in my life again, home from prison three years ahead of schedule. I really did have to get out of here.

9

I WAS COMING out the door into the cockpit when I saw Fontana's head sticking up over the transom. I said, "We need to talk," moving closer as I said it, seeing there was someone else beside him in the dinghy. The someone else was Julia Bonnell, in a Windbreaker and white tennis shorts.

"Let's talk later," Fontana replied, not smiling. He swung his feet over the gunwale and reached for a canvas gym bag Julia was handing him. "This is Matthew Shannon." He said it looking at Julia, who looked at me, nodding. Then he said, "Matthew, Julia Bonnell."

When Julia was standing in the cockpit, Fontana looked at me and back at her and asked, "I'm missing something, right?"

"Nice to see you again, Matt," Julia said.

"I'm not so sure."

"We bumped into each other at the Delano," she explained.

"I see," said Fontana.

"She's not going with us."

"Oh yes she is."

"Oh yes I am," Julia said.

Fontana was clearing the door to the salon, taking the gym bag with him. Julia yawned.

"I'm using the dinghy to get back to town," I announced.

"Fine," Fontana shot back. "Just do it in the next ten minutes because we need to get moving, with or without you. I'll be in my cabin."

Julia had followed him into the salon and sat down. Fontana was disappearing down the companionway stairs.

"This is a surprise," she said. "What on earth are you doing here?"

"You don't know?"

"I know as much as I want to. I'm just along for the ride."

"It's not the sort of thing you can just be along for the ride for."

"Why don't you go talk to Jack? You two seem to have a testosterone problem to work out."

I went down the companionway stairs into a corridor. The door to one of the cabins was open, and Fontana was sitting on a bunk with his eyes closed. He looked pale in the overhead light.

"I'm tired, Matt," he said.

When he opened his eyes I slapped him hard across the side of the face. He grabbed for the edge of the bunk but missed and went down on the floor. He put his arm up, waving me off, and got himself back against the wall.

When his breathing slowed down, he said, "Julia's a friend of mine who's going along to add camouflage. Two women on the boat is even better than one. If we get picked up, it'll look more convincing. She'll stay with Manuel in the Marquesas, then help him rendezvous with us when it's time."

"That's nice for us. She has no idea what she's getting into, does she? She could spend the next twenty years in prison."

"Not a chance. She doesn't even know enough to be an accessory after the fact."

"Then you should have told her."

"She wouldn't let me. Julia's not stupid." He looked

me in the eyes. "I should have let you know about her. I apologize."

"Not good enough. I want to know what else you haven't told me."

It was the wrong thing to say. He took his time starting to grin.

"You had me worried there, Matt. I thought you were going virtuous on me. You want to know who the money belongs to, that's really it."

True and not true.

"I already told you. It's not going to make any difference if I fill in the blanks, because you aren't going to know what it means, but here goes. The money belongs to Miriam Benages. She's in the import-export business in Miami. OK?"

He was right; the name meant nothing.

"A woman?"

"Technically, yes. If it makes you feel any better, Miriam Benages has a lot of men working for her. Manuel Rodríguez Colón used to be one of them. Her nephew. Look, it's nice we're having this conversation, but if we don't get moving very soon, it's all academic. You can take the dinghy back to town, but Julia's not going with you. You can stay, or you can go, but it's way too late in the game for this kind of bullshit. What I really need you to do is go up in the spotting tower so I can teach you some things about the boat. I'd like you to take a turn at the wheel between here and —"

Fontana had been trying to open the gym bag, but he didn't get to what he was looking for in time. He bent forward and threw up on the floor. What was on the floor was mostly liquid, some streaks of blood in it. He tried to say something and then bent over again, heaving. He had his fingers clenched around a handful of blanket. He sat up straight and took a deep breath.

"What the fuck is going on with you?"

"Seasick," he said. He unzipped the gym bag and got out a little kidney-shaped bowl. I recognized it from the hospitals, what the nurses called an emesis basin. He said, "I'll be up top in five."

I stood in the doorway for another moment and then went down the corridor. In the salon, at the top of the stairs, Julia was sitting with her legs folded on one of the settees, a glass of milk in one hand. A magazine lay on the cushion beside her, together with the stethoscope from her room at the Cardozo.

"He's throwing up," I said.

She got up very quickly and brushed past me down the companionway. I listened from the top of the stairs, but I couldn't hear anything coming from the cabin.

Outside in the cockpit I got a beer out of the cooler and looked at the dinghy for a while. I went so far as to untie the line from the cleat, then stopped, knowing I'd been conning myself.

I wasn't going back to town. A hundred good reasons existed for going, and a hundred bad ones for staying, but none of them mattered. I could tell myself I owed Fontana, and I did. I could say we were brothers, after all, in all but blood; there were all those electric nights and spiraling footballs. Or I could claim it was about her, Julia, and it was; that was a part of it. But my reasons for staying were spookier than that, and simpler. Fontana knew something about me I hadn't known till now in words: I needed to play this part to stay alive. He had called my bluff and won the hand. I tied the dinghy to the cleat and started climbing the tower.

The first thing I saw when I got up there was something the size of a cigarette pack wrapped in holiday paper and tied with a red ribbon. A playing card stuck out from beneath the ribbon: a jack of diamonds.

I tore the wrapping paper away and saw it was the black box, the gizmo that had disappeared from the patio three days ago. I rubbed it on my shirt and pitched it in the water.

Five minutes later Fontana walked forward along the side deck. He cast off the line from the mooring buoy, then came up the ladder into the spotting tower and started the engines, and we began moving toward the channel.

When we passed the *Empress* smoke was coming out of her stacks, and people were already on board looking over the rails, eager to get under way. One or two always got lost on Duval Street and didn't make it back in time, but many more were like these, the ones who couldn't wait to leave port, who probably didn't want to get off the ship in the first place.

At the last channel marker, Fontana put the *Ya-Ya* up on plane and set the autopilot. All I had to do was watch out for other boats, he said. Just stand there and watch and don't touch the wheel or the throttles unless we were about to run somebody over. After an hour, when I saw the nun buoy at Sampson Rock, I could cut the engines back to trolling speed and drive around in circles until he came back up to relieve me.

Krystal had left her Walkman on the bow, and Fontana had brought it with him up the ladder into the tower. He pulled a tape out of his pocket and handed it to me, yelling over the wind and the engines.

"In case you get bored! It's OK if you go down and get beer; just be sure to keep an eye out front of the bow."

I nodded. Key West was disappearing behind us. I could see the lights on top of the La Concha Hotel, that was about it. Up ahead was nothing but darkness, one or two fishing boats way off to the left.

"Matthew!"

"Yeah?"

"Why don't cannibals eat clowns?"

"What?"

"Why don't cannibals eat clowns?"

"I don't know. Why?"

"Because they taste funny!"

10

THE JOKE WAS connected to what was on the tape recording, but I didn't know that yet. When Fontana had gone down the ladder, I put the cassette in the Walkman and hit play. I was waiting for music, but what came through the earphones was a voice. The voice sounded far away and clear all at the same time. It was Kip, explaining how his hair had turned white. But I didn't know that yet either.

I stood in the spotting tower looking at the night beyond the *Ya-Ya*'s bow, hanging tight to the grab rails and listening.

"About a year later I ran into one of their drillers in Galveston, and he told me what happened before we got there," Kip's voice said. "Northstar Petroleum was ready to go in with some ex-Contra guys they had used in Honduras, but then these Catholic priests got wind of it. The head priest shows up at company headquarters in Manaus and gets down on his knees right there on the shag carpet and starts praying. The field director for Northstar, he's this Mick from Boston, he decides he's got nothing to lose. So he flies the priests up into the rain forest in one of the company choppers and drops 'em off, and the pilot says he'll be back in forty-eight hours to pick 'em up.

"So forty-eight hours later here comes the chopper. They took a few of the Honduran guys with rifles and grenades, so there's five of 'em total. The priests are there all right, right where they left them, but they got spears sticking out of their backs. It looked like the Indians had popped 'em in the forest pretty close by and then brought the bodies back to the clearing. The priests were sitting around in a little circle facing each other, like they were having a prayer meeting, except they were butt-naked with the spears stuck in their backs and coming out the front. Then all these arrows start hitting the chopper. One of the Hondurans got it through the neck. The others are firing into the forest, but they can't see a thing, even after they lift off and hightail it out of there.

"That's when we got involved. I guess the company figured the Hondurans weren't going to fill the bill.

Someone set a bulldozer on fire. The dozer operator was missing, and at first they thought he did it, but a few days later they found him drunk in Brasília and the thinking was: Indians again. I was out in Texas at the time.

"There was eight of us that came down, and North-star had all our equipment waiting for us: weapons, flash-bangs, all this high-tech tracking gear, and I'm like, shit, we're going hunting for little Third World midgets, right? What do we need this stuff for? They flew us up the Amazon to a base camp, and we pigged out on New York strips for a couple days. The compound had barbed wire around it, and they were drilling night and day all over the place, just mud and noise. These Contra fuckups were supposedly guarding the perimeter, but what they were really doing was watching MTV all day long in this tent they had set up. They pulled a hundred TV stations down off a satellite, and it was like black magic to these guys.

"We left out of there, and it was a long haul, hours. We had another Huey following behind us with extra fuel. Keep in mind, I didn't know about the priests at that point, so when we get to that clearing, to me it's just a bald spot on a hill. All the way in, it was nothing but jungle. We followed a river, the Negro, for the first hour or so, and once in a while you'd see a boat down there, but as soon as we turned north, there was nothing. I was hanging my feet out the gunner's door, and I kept looking down past my boots trying to find something besides jungle, but it was trees forever, man. No villages, no fields, no railroad tracks, no highways. Once I thought I saw something moving on a trail, but I couldn't be sure. I wasn't even sure there was really a trail. You couldn't see the ground, just the tops of trees, everything green. Pretty soon there were humps in one place, like little hills. That's where the clearing was, and now of course I understand why the guys in the other chopper were so fast getting the shit unloaded. Lagrange, the pilot, he wouldn't even get out. One of the Honduran guys refueled them from a fifty-five-gallon drum and then they were out of there, and it got real quiet.

"Northstar wanted these bad-ass Indians out of that part of the jungle so they could bring in their crews and start drilling. The priests had been doing their thing, see, trying to turn the Indians on to the baby Jesus. They thought they could talk 'em into moving farther north, but you saw what happened to that idea. There we were. It was seventeen thousand dollars a man for the job, and we figured it would take two or three days, so we were laughing our asses off. We set up watches and slept, and in the morning we took off and flew recon until we found their camp. We had three-month-old intelligence, and the camp turned out to be abandoned.

"The second day, more of the same thing. After about three hours we spotted smoke maybe fifty miles from the first camp. We flew right over, and you could see them running for cover. Our plan was to put down, get within a half mile of the place, and pound the shit out of 'em with a few mortar rounds and move in on foot. Nice idea. Like I said, you couldn't even see the ground, just treetops. There was absolutely no way to land the chopper. So we decide we're going to use the penetration anchor and slide ourselves down the fast rope. The pilot would take two guys and go back to the first camp we found, the abandoned one, and wait until we radioed for a pickup.

"OK. So we saddle up and go down the rope. Laos all over again, right? The chopper takes off, and the first thing we realize is there's no way we're using the mortar. We had a good fix on the village, that wasn't the problem. The problem was the trees again. Once you got down in there, you couldn't even see the sky. The trees were like a roof over your head, about eighty feet up. The only thing to do was to walk in.

"It was about an hour of bushwhacking until we picked up a trail. I'm figuring there's no way anyone's going to be left in that camp by the time we get there because of the racket we're making. I was wrong."

● ● ●

"The women and children were all there. We waited a long time before we went in, even though we knew they could see us hiding in the trees. They just stood there in front of their chickees, some of the women nursing babies. One of them would walk over and put a little piece of wood on the cook fire and then walk back.

"Now *we're* standing around. They're looking at us, and we're looking at them. What's the plan?

"Someone wanted to torch the place and call it a day, and someone else said that was no good, the Indians would just build a new camp, maybe right in the same place. The question got down to: where were the men? None of us spoke any Portuguese, and it didn't matter because these people had their own language. An old woman came out of one of the chickees and started yelling at us in it. Perez, he was half Mexican, he tries yelling back at her in Spanish, but neither one understands what the other's saying. The chickees were raised platforms with thatch roofs over the top but no walls, and when the old woman got done yelling, she climbed back up on her platform and lay down in a hammock.

"The only thing that made any sense was to wait there a while for the men to come back to camp, see if they were dumb enough to do that. We should have paid more attention when we flew over, because no one could really remember if we'd seen any men or not when everyone scattered. Which meant we didn't know if we had just happened to show up when they were off on business, or maybe they split when they heard the chopper. They could be sitting out there watching us right now.

"Lester and this guy James King, at this point they're both checking out one of the girls, getting ideas about some hammock action for themselves. The women weren't wearing anything but these little skirts, which was no big thrill because most of 'em were butt-ugly, real short and dumpy with bad teeth. This girl and maybe one other were all right. The next thing, Lester has her by one arm and James has the other, and they're walking off to the edge of the clearing. And what was weird is that no one seemed to care. The girl wasn't putting up a fight. The other women look bored, most of them already back under the thatch following Grandma's example.

"A little while later, Lester and James come back with the girl and big grins on their faces and say they got it figured out: the womenfolk are having their periods. The men go off hunting, like a ritual. What, they're *all* on the rag? Sure, says Lester, they get in sync. Happens all the time in sorority houses in Austin.

"I'm pretty wired at this point. This was back when I was eating a lot of crystal. What I'm starting to think is that one problem with our merry band is that no one's exactly in charge. We decide it would be a good idea to get on the radio and inform our chopper buddies what we're up to. Which we do, and they say fine, just keep in mind we need a couple hours of daylight to do a pickup and get back home. Otherwise we're stuck for the night, which nobody was counting on.

"A couple of the other guys want to take the girl out in the trees, but what we do instead is what we should have done from the get-go. The five of us spread out to the edge of the clearing, a few yards into the jungle, and wait, no talking, no smoking.

"Nothing happened. We sat there for seven hours. At four o'clock we gave up and threw all our gear in a pile in the middle of the camp. I got on the radio and started calling for the chopper, but there's no answer. Nothing. I popped in some fresh batteries: zip. We tried again every few minutes for an hour.

"At that point the only thing to decide is who's taking first watch. But the next morning we had some decisions to make. What we decided to do was torch the chickees and head east to the abandoned camp and the Huey.

"It took us two days to get there. It would have taken us a week if there hadn't been a clear trail the whole way. The first day we kept calling on the radio. The second day we just walked. You ever see that movie where those people get shrunk and they're in this little submarine going through the human body? That's what this was like. It was like moving through something that's alive. I mean, there were sounds coming from everywhere, especially at night. Things crashing through the trees way high up, other weird sounds all over the place, screams, grunts, you name it. Krystal gave me a book about the Amazon last year for Christmas. It says there's hundreds and hundreds of insect species that scientists haven't even named, and I believe it, on account of I met each one personally that first night, at least the ones that could fly and bite.

"We were not in a good mood when we got to the abandoned camp, but there was the chopper. At first I was happy to see it, but then it started to bother me. I had worked it out in my mind that Lagrange and the others had taken the bird back to the base camp for some reason that would make sense once I knew what it was. What didn't make sense was for them to be sitting here for two days with no food or water. If the receiver or the transmitter on their radio was screwed up, they would have figured it out pretty quick and come looking for us.

They had plenty of fuel. I climbed inside the chopper to check the radio, and it looked OK. It was there, anyway.

"What wasn't there was the crew. We had about three hours of light left. The first hour we just sat with our backs up against the chopper struts and relaxed. Lester spritzed a few rounds into the trees, and we waited some more, talking about what we were going to eat when we got somewhere with a restaurant. We would have lobbed some mortar rounds, but of course we had ditched the mortar along with the other heavy stuff the first day on the trail.

"There was still no sign of the chopper crew. Maybe they had gone off to find a stream and were on their way back right now after hearing the shooting. We were getting impatient, though, so when Perez found a game trail heading into the jungle on the other side of the camp, we figured that's the only way they could have gone. One or two of the guys wanted to sit tight with the chopper, but I knew this was no time for splitting up. Finally we all get up and head out, me walking point down the trail.

"About half a mile down, I stopped. I was really tired, more tired than I had realized, and I was coming off the crystal in a major way. I was turning around to say, 'This is ridiculous, fuck it,' when James King's gun goes off right behind me, full auto. What I see as I'm turning is this black guy backed up to a tree getting cut in half by rifle fire, the slugs hitting the tree trunk, *thap-thap-thap*. At the same time another black guy steps right out of nowhere onto the trail and shoves a spear through James King's back. The guy with the spear is wearing a Mickey Mouse T-shirt and a diaper. Lester's shooting it out with someone farther down the trail. I heard a sound behind me, and I'm spinning, clicking off my safety, and *KAPOW!* Something hits me hard and righteous. Everything goes to white pinwheels. That's it, lights out."

● ● ●

"WHEN I CAME TO, it was dusk, and I was sitting up against one of the chopper struts with the granddaddy of all headaches. I looked over and there was that same guy wearing the Mickey Mouse T-shirt and the diaper, a blue one. He was chewing the meat off a bone and looking at me. I looked back at him, and pretty soon it was like when you're a kid and you get in a staring contest with some other kid. Then he turned his head and said something to one of the others, and I realized he wasn't into the stare down at all. He was just looking at me, taking his time, wiping his fingers on Mickey Mouse. And right then I notice that what he's chewing on is a foot. Lester's foot, because Lester was the only guy with feet that big.

"Later on when I'm paying attention again, there's another one holding the end of a stick between his feet and twisting the stick around and around until it broke in two. I knew it wasn't a stick as soon as I saw it because it's got *Semper Fi* on the upper part, with a dagger and roses, but it still looked like a stick. It's like if you're ever in the woods at twilight thinking about bears, every other stump is going to look like one. Things look like what your mind wants them to look like, especially in certain kinds of light.

"Now *this* guy's looking at me. He raises up the smaller part of the arm and points it at me. There's some white bone sticking out the front. He's *offering* it. I shook my head, which doesn't mean anything to them, but I guess he got the point. I passed out again after that.

"I felt rain on my face and woke up, and it was dawn: red in the east over the clearing. Mickey Mouse is looking down at me, and he turns and says something to the others that I'm guessing means 'Breakfast is served.' I'm looking around for a gun, but there aren't any extras. I count six guys holding rifles, three more with just spears. I'm thinking, can I get inside the Huey and lock the doors and last long enough to get out of there, except I haven't flown a helicopter in years, and I can still only see out of one eye, and I'm pretty sure my collarbone is broken.

"What happened next: they're trying to get me on my feet, pissed off because I'm curled up in a ball, not wanting what's coming. They give up, and Mickey comes over and kicks me in the side. He starts screaming and pointing toward the western edge of the clearing, the trail, pointing and screaming. They got up and started walking, and so did I, one guy walking behind me to kick me in the ass from time to time if I didn't keep pace. He would yell up to the front of the line every once in a while, and some of the others would yell back.

"I thought I would pass out, but I didn't, and the next night we walked into camp. The women were all there, and I could see they had started rethatching the chickees. Grandma comes out to the center of the clearing and kicks me in the leg, hard. I go down on the ground, and I figure, OK, that's it: I *know* these guys are hungry after walking nonstop for a day and a half. But I was wrong again. Nobody ate a thing. Everyone lay down and went to sleep. I was surprised I slept, but I did.

"The next day what woke me up was gunshots and screaming. I figured someone had shot someone else with one of the Kalashnikovs, but it was just Mickey, scared shitless but pleased with himself for figuring out how to click off the safety.

"That's when I saw my chance. I went over and started showing him how to hold the gun, how to snug it up to his shoulder, how to sight down the barrel. I showed him how to load and unload. By the end of the day I had those guys doing basic infantry drills, maneuvers for close combat, mock firefights — what a trip! After a couple more days, some of them left camp and went to gather up all the ammo clips we had dumped our first time down the trail.

"One night I woke up, and there was a face. It was the girl, the one Lester and James King had taken out in the trees. She was squatting down, watching me. What woke me up was her hand touching my hair. After a while she put her hand on my hair again, and then she got up and went away.

"It might have been three months that went by. My eye and the rest of me healed up, and I learned some of their words, but not many. I could say hi to Grandma, but she wouldn't say anything back. It had something to do with the girl. The girl didn't have any kids, and it seemed like a problem for her. Several times at night I would wake up and she would be there, squatting down, watching and waiting. Finally I just said to hell with it and fucked her, and after that she left me alone. Yeah, yeah, I know, but I did.

"Needless to say, my homies ran out of ammunition. The huts were all done now. Things would have been boring, except that every so often the men would go off on these walks, and I was expected to go along with them.

"These guys could walk, man. I mean, some days we must have walked thirty miles, and that's through serious terrain. I would be stumbling and crawling and running sometimes trying to keep up, and I knew if I didn't stay with them it was all over. Sometimes *they* got lost, like for days. You couldn't tell at first, because it didn't seem like they cared one way or another whether they knew where they were going. The worst thing was, they didn't eat when they were on these hikes, and we're talking a week or ten days at a time, easy. Once when I was pretty sure they were lost, we came to a river and they sat down and waited for a day and a night until some guys in canoes came along. I was thinking: what now, they're gonna jump these mothers? But they didn't. They got directions from them. They also got a shitload of food, little jungle pigs stretched on sticks that were all piled up in the canoes. I couldn't believe it, because it didn't seem like the guys in the canoes got anything in return. They were practically cleaned out. Then everyone starts eating, and it goes on for like three hours. They almost ate everything. I swear to God, they must have eaten twenty pounds of meat apiece. By then it was night, and everyone passed out like they'd been boozing. It was fucking incredible.

"But it wasn't as incredible as the next trip, because on that one, we're walking through the jungle again, and the next thing I know there isn't any more jungle. We walked out into a clearing about three miles wide, and it almost blinded me. There was a road, and we got on it and kept walking and after a while along came a bus. I'm like, what the fuck? These cannibals are going to town? And that's exactly what happened. We all got on the bus. One of them gave his walking stick to the driver. To me it looked like a stick, but the driver acted like it was a case of Dom Perignon. The closer we got to the city the more the bus filled up, people trying to stay cool with these cannibals on board.

"We drove downtown, and they all got up at the same time and made the bus driver stop at a certain street. The street was mud, but there was a concrete sidewalk. Mickey gets out, he bends down and knocks on the sidewalk with his knuckles and stands up and starts laughing like it was the funniest thing on earth. They all head for the doorway of this store, and just when the last one gets through it, I started running down the street big-time. I didn't stop running till I came to a harbor. I found the captain of a river ferry who could speak English, and he explained to me how to get out of there.

"Anyway, you asked, so I told. I slipped into the bathroom at the airport to take some money off this guy who looked like a professor. I glanced over at the mirror and freaked out. My hair was totally white."

There was a long pause. Then it was Manny talking.

"So from all of this you learned that retirement would be best?"

"You're a dipshit, Manny. You missed the whole point of the story. What I learned? What I learned is I am what I am and a tree is what a tree is. The point is to keep on being it as long as you can. Those guys were cannibals, so they ate my pards. They were doing what a cannibal's supposed to do."

"They didn't eat you."

"Right," Kip said. "That's the part I never quite figured out."

There was nothing, and then there was the sound of bedsprings creaking.

"Manny," said Kip's voice, much softer, "I flat-out love it when you do that."

11

I WAITED, BUT there was no more story, just a low hum
on the tape recording. Something went blink way out
at one o'clock, and I figured: masthead light on a sailboat
or a shrimper coming home from the Dry Tortugas. I
kept the Walkman on my head and let the hum keep
going while I climbed down from the spotting tower
and dug in the ice chest. In the tower you had to hang on
tight or get pitched against the grab rails. Down here
there was less rock and roll but more spray and more engine noise. I stepped up on the side deck to check the
view and caught a face full of saltwater off the top of a
swell. No more blinks up ahead, though.

No light at all, except the red and green running
lights on the bow and the glow coming through a nar-

row strip of window halfway between me and the bow pulpit. I knelt before I had a chance to fall down, and then I started crawling forward with the beer in my hand. The closer I got to the bow, the more the hull pounded against the swells, and the harder it was to hold on. A stiff breeze was blowing out of the southeast, with plenty of spray coming over the side. Soon I was soaked, but I didn't care. I had a good buzz going off the beer, and even with the wind, the water felt warm. Veins of warm water streamed across the window strip, and the light coming through the watery glass was warm too, a golden glow.

I lay flat while the boat bucked and got my face down close to the glass. Fontana was on his side a few feet below me with his knees pulled up and his arms folded. I could see plastic tubing coming from somewhere else in the cabin and leading to a square of gauze on his chest. He folded his arms tighter, shaking, and then I guessed he had said something. Julia's hand and arm appeared and next the back of her head. She threw her hair over one shoulder and got hold of a little rubber port that branched off the IV tubing. Her other hand came into view, holding a syringe with a needle. She sank the needle into the rubber port and began pushing the plunger on the syringe. She was taking her time with it, and before she got done and pulled the needle out,

Fontana had stopped shaking. He reached up and took her hand in his and put it against his cheek.

I was leaning back on one elbow to take another swallow out of the beer bottle when I saw the buoy. It was about the size of a station wagon and was coming up sideways, righting itself from where it wallowed in the trough of a swell directly in front of the *Ya-Ya*'s bow. I grabbed the nearest stanchion, and the beer bottle went skittering back down the side deck toward the cockpit. The buoy's signal light flashed on, throwing white light over the deck. After a long moment there was darkness again, and after that the sudden slamming and shrieking as the buoy hit the fiberglass hull and started dragging under the boat. The *Ya-Ya* seemed to rear up on its side. Then the crisscross metal top of the buoy came shooting past my left shoulder in a rush of foam as the signal light flashed on again. Down inside the blinding light was a hard jerk and a chunking sound. My head had smacked against the deck, and I couldn't decide whether the chunking sound was inside my head or outside, something ripping loose and giving way under the stern. The engine noise had dropped off and changed pitch, but the boat was still moving. I looked behind me and saw the buoy falling out of sight, already forty feet back.

I had stood up and begun moving toward the stern but then dropped down into a crouch. Another boat, only a few yards away, was running alongside the *Ya-Ya*. Mixed up with the saltwater taste I had the coppery taste of blood now, and one eye was blurry with water or blood or both. It was another moment before I realized that the person standing in the pilothouse doorway on the other boat was Manny and that the boat was Kip's lobster boat. Manny was shaking his head and laughing.

The *Ya-Ya* pitched and rolled in the swells, almost dead in the water. When I got to the cockpit Fontana was coming down the ladder from the spotting tower wearing a pair of boxer shorts with little blackjack hands printed on them.

"Look," he said, turning around. "Considering how we're on our way to commit a carefully orchestrated international incident and all, maybe it's time to knock off the drinking."

I got a fresh beer out of the cooler and sat down on the lid. "Fine," I said.

Fontana looked at me with his hands on his hips, smiling. His pupils were pinpoints. "How'd you like the tape?" he asked.

I looked around. The Walkman was gone.

"Don't worry, I've got another copy," he said. "It's a collector's item."

"Let me guess. That's what you're using to blackmail Manny."

Fontana laughed and kept laughing until he started coughing. As he sat down on the bait cooler next to me, Julia stepped off the side deck into the cockpit. She started to say something but changed her mind. I noticed a line connecting the *Ya-Ya* to Kip's lobster boat. Manny was waiting until the swells brought the two close enough together to jump on board.

"Come downstairs," Julia said, meaning me.

I sat on the berth in Fontana's cabin looking at the IV rig while Julia numbed my eyebrow. She threaded a needle and frowned while she started sewing in sutures.

"All that stuff about me being a high-priced hooker was something Jack dreamed up. It was an act. We thought it would help draw you in."

"Terrific," I said. "It worked. What about your sugar baron? And what's-his-name?"

She shrugged. "Friends of Jack's, playing a part. I thought you suspected it was a scam. Or had figured it out by now. I'm afraid the truth isn't very exotic. I work in the ICU at Abbott Northwestern in Minneapolis. I have an herb garden. I'm in a book group. I'm sorry I deceived you."

"OK," I said. "But why?"

"Jack said you were a sucker for damsels in distress. Hold still."

"No, I mean why draw me in at all?"

"That's obvious, isn't it?" She looked into my eyes before going back to the sutures. "He wants to show you some things. He thinks you've got nothing to lose, and it seems like you agree with him because here you are."

I wondered if she knew what the others knew, how Fontana had taken the fall for me, eaten my sin. Or what the others didn't know, about a black box lying under Key West harbor, another lever he had used, or decided not to. She finished with the stitches and started putting things away in a plastic box.

"What's killing him?"

She laughed. "The same thing that's killing you, Matt. Life. Mileage. In his case, a little too much of it. But the difference between you and Jack is that he didn't wake up one morning and decide to call it quits. He'd prefer to be alive. He is alive. I'm not so sure about you."

"I'm not sure what we're talking about."

She glanced at the beer in my hand. Then she looked away. "What's killing Jack. Every hospital I've worked in has the same euphemism for it: fever of unknown origin. It doesn't matter what's killing him. What matters is that instead of spending his remaining days in an AIDS hospice, he decided to make his own sort of last stand. He wants to show you a way to start over, even if it's too late for him. He doesn't care about the money. The money's for you. You and me. He wants us to be provided for when he's gone. Do you remember the fox?"

"The fox?"

"Coming back in the dinghy this afternoon, Jack told me a story about when you two were boys. You don't remember what happened in the tree house?"

"No, I don't. That was a long time ago."

"Well, yes. It was a long time ago, and you don't remember. I'm afraid that's the point."

I could tell she was about to stand up. I reached across the space between us and put my hand on hers.

"I don't understand what you are to him."

"His nurse, at the moment."

"What else?"

She took her hand away. She stood up and turned toward the door and then turned back again and looked at me. "You really don't get it yet, do you?"

I hadn't heard Fontana come down the stairs. He appeared in the doorway suddenly enough to startle me.

"After much arm-twisting, Manuel went over the side with a flashlight," he said. "We've lost one propeller but the other one's fine. So we're OK. And now it's time to go."

12

IT WAS FONTANA who first caught sight of her, a white
gleam on the black horizon, dull at first but soon distinct, tinged with reds and blues, a whole. The glow beneath the radar hood showed a small green streak, the
same ship we saw with our eyes eight miles ahead in the
darkness.

Fontana had picked a night with a crescent moon to
run under, but it hardly mattered. The sea was filled
with shadows thrown down from an overcast sky. Even
a full moon wouldn't have changed its heaviness. The
Marquesas lay forty miles behind us now, with Manny
and Julia waiting at anchor there aboard the *Ya-Ya*.

Fontana slowed and then cut the engines and stood
in the cockpit of Kip's lobster boat with the backwash

slapping and sloshing over the transom. He looked at the gear strapped and chained on deck and then looked at me. Neither one of us said anything. When he restarted the engines I noticed the red and green running lights had gone dark, and then Fontana was giving me the wheel, waiting to do it until the prow rode over the top of a swell.

We came at her in a wide semicircle from the east, and she was all color now, a blaze of neon with one big string of white lights along the top from bow to pilothouse, across the stacks and down to the stern. Flickers and blinks, flashes and glows, but silent. It was too soon to see the bow or stern wakes cutting white foam out of the black water. At two miles we slowed and stopped again, letting the engines idle while we loaded the weapons and got out the masks.

"OK," Fontana said. "This is it."

He reached for the handheld radio and kept punching the roamer key until he got channel 4. I checked my watch.

"Another three minutes," I said.

There was no radio traffic on 4. The ship was moving along a line parallel to us. Miles ago the mate would have picked us up on his own radar, perhaps even noticed when we stopped. He would think: just another fishing boat crossing an unmarked highway, pulling in close to gawk at his sideways skyscraper.

"Now?"

I watched the hands on my wristwatch, raising one of my own in a gesture of patience. Then I said: "OK."

"OK, what?"

"Midnight. Midnight on the dot."

"Sea Rover to Rasta Mon," Fontana said. He spoke in a conversational tone.

A pause.

"Sea Rover to Rasta Mon," he repeated.

"Rasta Mon. Go to low power." It was Bryant.

Fontana toggled the power switch, dropping the signal down so it could be picked up only at close range.

Bryant came back on and said, "All right. Party time."

We had already lost some distance on the ship. Fontana checked the radar and reported, "We're at three miles. Coming in fast on your port side. Do it."

"We're doing it. Go."

And then we were flying, up on plane, smashing through the swells toward where the ship would cross our bow. I put the radio on 16. At one mile it crackled to life, and a voice came on, hailing us. The voice waited a few seconds and then tried again in Spanish, then two more times in English, the last time with some urgency.

We kept going, and I switched back over to 4 and waited, the volume turned up high. Bryant would have his own hand-held clipped to his flak jacket, the transmitter locked open so we could hear what happened next.

It came when we were a quarter mile off the ship's bow, and I was getting a sense of her size. I could see passengers, just a few, leaning against the rail on the promenade deck or walking along beside the railing toward the stern.

The next words that came through the radio were Kip's. There was no sense of the pilothouse door opening, just Kip saying: "Don't touch anything. Not anything. Be cool, that way no one gets dead."

Then Krystal saying, "Step back from the console and get down on your knees. Hands behind your necks. Right NOW! Cross your ankles!"

"You're making a serious mistake," a voice responded.

There was a sudden scream that stopped just as suddenly.

"Anyone else want some 'lec-tricity?" Bryant said. "Hey! YOU! Who are you?"

"Second mate." The voice was quiet, almost muffled. It sounded young.

"OK, second mate. I want you to get the captain up

here on the double. Do it how you normally do it. Stand up. You do this right or it's the last thing you ever do."

Half a minute passed.

"Down, boy!" Bryant barked. "Get back down there!"

We had turned alongside the ship and kept running with her at almost twenty knots. Three passengers on the promenade deck were cheering, waving big plastic cups. Fontana waved back at them. We were only fifteen yards from the side of the ship, but they were too high up to really make us out.

Right now I could picture Krystal standing next to the radio room holding one of the guns on the radio officer. Bryant and Kip would be waiting by the door for the captain to walk through.

A sudden, furious crashing erupted from the radio.

"Don't move!" Bryant screamed. "Don't MOVE, motherfucker!"

And that was it. I heard a zipping sound, Kip or Bryant putting plastic handcuffs on the captain and the mate and the radio officer. The next thing that would happen would be the third engineer calling up to the bridge to say ha-ha, very funny, it seemed someone had padlocked all the hatches leading in and out of the engine room.

I managed to light a cigarette, bending down under the console, and when I had half smoked it, I saw that the *Empress* was slowing down.

13

I T TOOK THE SHIP more than three miles and nine minutes to come to a complete stop. Then it started moving again, regaining momentum until it held at around four knots. The breeze had died, and the sea was a dead flat calm, which turned out to be a very good thing.

I watched from the stern of the lobster boat as Krystal appeared above me on the promenade deck, dragging the Jacob's ladder. She clipped one end to the railing and barely got the coiled bulk over the side. It unrolled down four stories, the last of the ladder rungs splashing in the foam.

I wanted things to slow down so I could think, but I was already reaching for the ladder, my arms chafing against the Kevlar vest, my breath warm and wet on the inside of my Ronald Reagan mask.

As soon as I had both feet on one of the wooden ladder rungs and my hands on the two ropes that supported them, Fontana backed the lobster boat away from the ship. I took a step, then another, looking up for a shadow or hollow that would give away what I was looking for. After a few more steps, I saw it: the butt of a hinge on one of the galley cargo doors, the thing I would use as an anchor. I tried to get the mooring line into a better position between my teeth and nearly lost it. Then I was in reach of the hinge.

Above me the steel walls of the ship rose straight up into darkness. I wrapped my left arm around the left ladder rope and tied the nylon line to the rung just above me. Then I took two of the plastic handcuffs from my belt and laced them through the back of the hinge, closed them into a loop, and tied the mooring line to the doubled handcuffs.

I heard a burst of laughter and saw three heads in silhouette looking over the railing, a pair of arms waving. More laughter, a whoop, then a plastic cup falling through shadows and hitting the side of the ship. Below me Fontana was standing on the bow of the lobster boat reaching out for the ladder, the muzzle of his rifle knocking against steel.

The lobster boat bumped the ship, then drifted back a few feet, taking up slack in the mooring line. I got ready to climb again and pulled the mask down over my face. Up: toward the starless sky, the ladder more stable now with Fontana's weight on it.

Where the twin ropes of the Jacob's ladder disappeared over the railing far above me I could see Krystal's head, with a flashlight next to it. The beam followed me as I reached for the next rung and reached again. I stopped in front of a rectangular window, a porthole, and looked in. A shirtless fat man lay on a bed reading a book. A door opened, and a woman in a nightgown came out of a bathroom.

My hand found one of the airline bottles in my pocket. I unscrewed the top and drank it in one swallow, feeling the dark, liquid thrill go all the way down my throat. I let go of the bottle and watched it fall past my feet into darkness.

The man closed his book and started turning just as the woman glanced at the window.

I reached for the next rung and took a step up, and then all at once I'm in another place, going up a rope ladder to the tree house a lifetime ago in Etna Furnace. Jack's ahead of me, climbing toward the stars, toward Orion overhead and the Dipper on my right. I go up the ladder into the tree house and see the still-warm body of the fox stretched out on the floor in moonlight. Jack sits Indian-style with his pocketknife beside him saying, *"The fox lives on the edge of things. He stays out of sight, but he's always watching."* He picks up the knife and frowns as he cuts at his finger, saying like an incantation: *"The fox will trade himself for his family, if it comes to that. But he doesn't let it come to that. That's what redemption is."* I watch him touch the knife to the creature's throat, the silver blade part moonlight and part blood when he raises it in the trembling air between us.

I kept climbing. The three figures were still there off to my right and above me on the promenade deck. "Dude!" one of them hollered. "Hey! I'm sorry I dropped my beer on your head!" A combination of hilarious giggling and *shh*-ing from the other two. "Shut up, you fucking gomer!" another voice said. "The guy's gonna pop your ass!" By now they could see the guns.

Then, right then, and quicker than I would have thought it could happen, the rope in my left hand tore and parted with a musty snap, and I was falling backward, flailing and kicking in my jumpsuit out into darkness. The next thing was not falling but hitting. Pain shot through my knee, and my head and shoulder hit steel as one leg caught with a jerk in the crook of a rung, my whole weight hanging from the one unbroken ladder rope. For a long moment I was nailed to the side of the ship, my arms splayed out below me and the heel of my free leg kicking and clawing. Upside down and crucified, I might have thought, but there was no thinking then, not in any human way. I sensed the mindless ocean as I hung and swung above it; not consciously, not with just one part of me, but wholly. The rifle slipped from my shoulder and fell, but at the last possible moment, I caught the strap by my fingertips.

The lobster boat followed beside the ship, tethered to it with the mooring line and bouncing gently against the blue bumpers Fontana had set between the two vessels. I heard a shout and looked down, upside down. Fontana clung to the Jacob's ladder with both arms, the wooden rungs collapsed between us, and the one remaining ladder rope turning and twisting, ready to go.

So this is it, I thought. I felt the pain in my shoulder and tried to breathe, my cheek turned to the cold of the ship and my heart beating with it. This is it then. I heard the roaring of the sea that was my own blood and thought I saw specks of phosphorescence in the low swells forty feet below me. You could let go now, I thought.

I became aware of the wheeze and whistle of breath going in and out of my lungs. A star appeared in a hole made of clouds in the corner of my eye, then a second one; then a whole unnamed constellation that I alone had discovered and would keep my secret. Panic was near me, but with it was something else. I was inside and out of myself, rising up in sunlight in some other place as I never had in my waking life. But I was right here. There was nowhere except where I was, and I was in it, deeply. I opened my eyes. I thought to pray, and let my body do it.

My leg had steadied itself, the heel against the side of the ship. But the other one, the one I hung from, had started to shudder and twitch. I concentrated everything and brought the rifle strap up to my neck and over my chin, hooking it there. My hands moved like independent things, inching up the face of the ship that was as smooth as the milled stone of a monument; I could see them in my mind's eye, like a movie close-up. The feeling in my bowels and groin was unmistakable, a sexual keening that shocked me. I curled into myself with everything I had and, reaching up, gripped the one good rope with my right hand.

I sat and finally stood in the collapsed crook of the rung that had saved me, and after what seemed like a long time, I started up the rope, arming it out to the next rung, the next standing spot, shaking badly. I got beyond where the ladder had broken and watched Fontana rising hand over hand through the place I had come from, across the void in the ladder between the shadows and the intact upper rungs. I wondered if this was what he had had in mind.

As soon as I brought my head over the railing I heard music from somewhere inside the ship. The silhouettes I had seen belonged to three frat boys. They were leaning on the railing, not saying anything now, just grinning and trying to look relaxed. I stood there, breathing hard and shaking off the feeling of a dream.

Fontana was still ten yards down the ladder. I took the flashlight from Krystal and held it on him, and he looked up at me for a moment before he went back to climbing. He had thrown up down the front of his flak vest.

I could tell one of the frat boys was trying to say something. He cleared his throat. "Uh. What are you guys doing?" All three of them wore clean T-shirts and baseball caps over short haircuts. Krystal was looking at them from behind her Wonder Woman mask. I kept the light on Fontana. The boy tried again. "I mean, do you need any help?"

Fontana's hand reached up and connected with mine. I could see blood on the front of his vest. So could the college boys. They didn't say anything. I held and held, drawing him up the ladder rungs, and saw it then inside me, the rest of what had happened in the tree house forty years ago: saw myself take the knife out of the trembling air and cut across my palm in moonlight and take Jack's hand, joining with the fox's blood, and his.

He took it slow coming over the rail. I gripped him by the arm, and then when he was steady on his feet, I took my hand away and we looked at each other through our masks.

He unclipped the Jacob's ladder and let it fall away down the side of the ship into darkness. The frat boys looked over the side and so did I. The lobster boat was still there, dimly, the nylon line white in the white light, anchoring the boat to the hinge on the ship's cargo door.

And then we were moving. We walked quickly, Fontana leading, Krystal next. The deck on this part of the ship was narrow. A lifeboat hung nearby. Farther toward the bow was a young couple holding hands who turned and watched us pass by, not saying anything. Very fast, we turned into a doorway and moved through a carpeted lobby, going toward a broad stairway with brass rails. Near the bottom of the stairway was a reception desk like in a hotel, but no one was behind it. As I started up the stairs I glanced through the double doors of a ballroom where music was blaring. I could see small, round tables lit with candle lanterns, shapes of people on a dance floor.

Bryant was waiting at the top of the stairway. We followed him down a short corridor and up some steps to the bridge. He knocked and said, "It's me," and Kip un-locked the door. We walked into the pilothouse.

The radio officer and chief mate lay on the floor, hog-tied with riot strips. The captain, looking serious, was over on the left, standing with his hands behind his back. His hair was ruffled up into a rooster tail. Kip sat in the big padded pilot's chair with his AR-14 on the captain.

"Key to the holding cell," Fontana said. He sounded calm under the mask.

The captain brought his hands out from behind his back and raised them to his side, palms up, and started to say something, maybe something about international laws against locking up crew members. Fontana's rifle butt caught him in the stomach, and he went down on the floor with a squawk. Fontana rolled him onto his side and got his hand in his pocket, coming up with a key ring. He held it in front of the old man's face. The captain was starting to cry, but he reached out and showed Fontana the key, a little silver one.

Bryant took one of the riot strips from his belt and fas-tened the captain's hands behind his back and then used his knife to cut the plastic from around the ankles of the other officers. We got them on their feet.

"Mate's sidearm?" Fontana asked.

"Over the side," Kip said.

Fontana looked past him to where he must have thrown it: the compass bridge beyond a storm door.

"You realize that our unexplained stop has by now been reported to the Coast Guard." It was the chief mate. Fontana ignored him. We knew we had time. Or some time.

Kip, Krystal, and I took the rear, behind the hand-cuffed officers. Fontana and Bryant led the way down a steep service stairway, five flights, as fast as they could go. Halfway down I heard a shout, and when I could see past Fontana to the next landing, a stocky man in a white uniform was lying on his side. Bryant had set his Taser on the landing and was going through the guy's wallet.

"First engineer," he told Fontana.

Bryant handcuffed the man, who was coming to. It took him only a few seconds, and while he worked he kept an eye on the chief mate. We had both figured out he was the one to watch. The engineer struggled to his feet and stumbled down the stairs to the next level, Bryant holding him by the back of the collar and nearly running with him.

The door we were after was down a hallway that split off along a bulkhead. Bryant opened it using the cap-tain's key.

Inside the room there was a little black man sitting on

the edge of a bunk. He wore tan coveralls and had been reading a book that looked like some sort of religious text written in a foreign language. A wreath of hand-cuffs and leg irons hung from the corner of the top bunk, but the little man wasn't wearing any restraints. He looked puzzled but got up quickly and moved out into the corridor when we motioned for him.

After the officers filed inside the room, Fontana closed the door and locked it, testing the door handle. Kip had pulled off his mask.

"Put that back on," Fontana ordered. He was already moving down the hallway, the short rifle slung under his arm. "Go get the others," he said as he brushed past Bryant. The others meant the purser, the chief steward, the second engineer, and the executive chef, who had been a combat marine. One or two others. Then he looked at me and said, "Let's go find Menoyo." He glanced at his watch, shaking his head.

14

MENOYO WAS SITTING next to a dough mixer in the middle of the galley. When we took off our masks, he laughed.

"Scary monsters," he said. "Look, after you tie me up, don't put me in the cooler, OK? It's freezing in there. I frostbit both my hands when I was a kid, and they still give me fits."

"Let's take a look at the money," said Fontana.

Menoyo walked with us through the galley and pulled open the door of a stockroom. Inside were three shipping pallets. Each pallet held about forty cases of what looked like powdered milk. Fontana motioned to me, and I cut through the polyurethane that covered the boxes and tore one of them open. It was powdered milk.

"Try the next one down," Menoyo said, a little nervous.

I did, and inside was currency, jammed and mashed together into a big brick sealed in thick plastic.

Fontana lit a cigar and walked out to the galley loading bay, taking a moment to figure out how the cargo doors opened. He looked pale. Overhead was a retractable hoist designed to stick out over the side of the ship and winch materials up and through the cargo doors. Fontana was leaning against a prep counter. He had put out the cigar.

"You're going to have to do this," he said without turning his head.

I got the cargo doors unlocked and swung them back against the side of the ship. The lobster boat was off to the right, ten feet down and running along on its mooring line, snug against the bumpers. The chop had picked up, and some of the swells almost reached the lower edge of the doors.

Menoyo was using a pallet jack to bring the first pallet across the galley. I spotted a boat hook hanging by a cord and used it to get hold of the mooring line fastened to the hinge outside.

"Don't try to untie it," Fontana directed. "Just cut it. We need to pick up the pace."

I cut the line and started hauling on it, bracing against

the doorway. It came easier than I expected, and soon I had the bow of the lobster boat snugged up to the door.

"Tie it off and get on board," Fontana said, "then connect the winch cable."

"To the Dumpster?"

"No. To the welders. Bring the welders up first, both at once if you can. Then hand up one of the machine guns. After that we'll work on the Dumpster."

I got the hoist boom out over the side of the ship, positioned above the lobster boat, and then found the cable release for the winch and dragged the steel hook down from the ceiling. When the next swell brought the bow up to the edge of the doorway, I eased myself quickly onto the wet deck of the lobster boat. The cable kept unspooling as I went down.

I got on all fours and crawled back to the cockpit and hooked the cable through the handle of one arc welder and then through the handle of the other. I felt a thrill of excitement then. We were making it work. I could see Fontana in the doorway. He turned the switch on the hoist, and the cable ran taut and started lifting the welders. They dragged out of the cockpit and up over the gunwale of the lobster boat, hung in the air, and kept going. Fontana fiddled with the control box, and then the welders started moving on runners until they passed through the galley cargo doors. He unhooked them and rolled them to the side, out of sight. Then he hit the cable release and spooled out slack until he could hand me down the hook.

I made my way back along the deck from the bow of the lobster boat and got the plastic tarp off the Dumpster. It had started to rain. I looked up, expecting to see heads peering down from the quarterdeck, but nobody was there. I uncoupled the chains that held the empty Dumpster in place. As soon as I got the last chain free and attached the cable, I motioned, and the cable started reeling in. The sound changed when the weight caught, but the hoist kept lifting the Dumpster evenly off the deck. It banged the gunwale, tearing off a section of the rub rail as it dragged over the side, then swung hard, its bottom hitting the water. But it kept rising.

I dragged the .50 caliber machine gun behind me toward the bow, and when I looked, Bryant and Krystal were standing in the doorway guiding the Dumpster into the cargo bay. Bryant reached out and got hold of the gun and pulled it through the doorway. The bow of the lobster boat reared and slammed against the side of the ship, and I grabbed the edge of the doorway and got through it in one motion.

When I stood up, I was looking past Kip and Fontana at Neal Atlee walking toward us down the length of the galley. He looked at me and stopped. His mouth opened to say something, but then he began moving again.

He looked terrified. His eyes were wide open.

"You're not supposed to be here," Fontana said.

Atlee didn't say anything for a moment. He glanced at me and started rubbing one hand against his shoulder as though worrying an old injury. "She's here," he said. "On board."

No one said anything. Then Fontana asked: "Who is on board?"

"Who the fuck do you think?" Atlee almost screamed. "Miriam Benages!"

15

IT DOESN'T MATTER," Fontana said, not looking at Atlee. Then he glanced at him. "You're afraid, aren't you?"

"You're fucking goddamn right I'm afraid," Atlee yelled. "This wasn't part of the plan. She'll take one look at me and know I'm involved. She could roll in here any second to check on that shit." He cut his eyes toward the pallets. Menoyo had brought the third one over and was leaning against the pallet jack, watching.

"And see you standing here," Fontana said. "Where you aren't supposed to be."

"Uh," Menoyo interrupted, "can I get tied up now? If you don't tie me up, they'll know I was in on it."

"No," Fontana said. "Start loading the boxes into the Dumpster." He was still looking at Atlee. "Wait a minute. I want you to see something. Both of you."

Fontana walked over to the open cargo doors. Atlee followed, then Menoyo.

"Neal. Who does she have with her?" Fontana said.

Atlee laughed. "Three guys. They all have mustaches."

After a moment Fontana asked: "What do you see out there?"

"Out there?"

"Yes. Out there."

"You mean the boat?" Atlee was looking down at Kip's lobster boat, keeping his distance from the edge of the doorway.

"No, not the boat. Just out there in general."

Atlee took his time looking out the cargo doors. When he spoke he sounded annoyed, but also nervous. "I don't see anything out there. I see nothing. Darkness."

"Right," Fontana said. "It's the way I imagine heaven to be."

I felt sick then. Fontana brought the pistol up from his side very quickly and put it next to Atlee's head. Then he pulled the trigger. My ears rang. Atlee was lying in the doorway then, and Menoyo was screaming. He had fallen on top of Atlee, but he got up fast.

Fontana put the gun in his shoulder holster and looked around. He took the boat hook off the wall and untied the cord it hung from. Then he bent down and tied one end of the cord around Atlee's left ankle. He carried a meat slicer over from the counter nearby, set it on the floor, and then tied the other end of the cord around the slicer and pushed it through the doorway with his foot. Atlee flopped over and dragged through the doorway and disappeared into the darkness. Menoyo had stopped screaming. Part of Atlee was on his shirt.

"Get started with the welders," Fontana said.

• • •

WE BEGAN AT THE STERN and hit the movie theater first. I peeked inside and saw Jamie Lee Curtis on the screen trying to scramble out a basement window that was too small for her. The theater wasn't even half full. I had taken off one mask and put on another: a welder's mask. I plugged the arc welder into a socket and put a fresh rod in the clamp. It took about thirty seconds to get a good bead most of the way down the double doors and weld them shut. There wasn't much for Bryant to do while I worked at sealing up the theater. Kip and Krystal were four decks down, using the other welder to seal the hallways leading to the crew quarters. Fontana had said he would check the engine room and the holding cell, giving us notice on the radio before he moved on.

The ship had only one passenger elevator, one elevator shaft. The doors opened and inside was an elderly couple, all dressed up. I got in. Bryant wheeled the welder in. The doors closed. I could feel the old man looking at me. I was dripping with sweat.

"We've stopped moving, haven't we?" the old lady said. "The ship?"

I didn't say anything. Bryant said, "We'll be under way shortly, ma'am. Just a minor mechanical problem involving the starboard turbine. Here." He had dug in his pocket and come up with a pair of tablets. "Dramamine. Are you feeling seasick from the swells?"

She nodded. "It's worse when we're not moving, isn't it?" She took the tablets from Bryant.

"Yes, ma'am."

"Are you part of the comedy troupe?"

Bryant nodded. He bent forward and brought his hand up to his lips, speaking in a stage whisper. "We're the understudies."

"Oh!" she exclaimed. "May I have your autograph?"

"Most certainly," Bryant said.

She handed him a playbill, and he signed it. When he gave it back to her, she handed it to me. I wrote *John Smith* in big cursive.

"We're going to lie down in our cabin," the old man said. The elevator stopped, and the doors opened. I hit the red toggle.

"Happy Halloween!" Bryant called out.

When the couple was thirty feet away, he closed the hallway fire doors behind them, and I started welding. We kept going, doing the same thing to the fire doors on each side of the elevator shaft on every level, sealing off the passengers and crew, anyone who wasn't awake and moving around in the public places of the ship. It was necessary, and it went pretty quickly, but still not fast enough, I thought. The amount of time it was taking worried me, even as my heart pounded, even as I caught myself smiling just a bit behind the mask, excited and going with it.

From the bottom of the ship we rode the elevator back to the quarterdeck. I got the control box open with a pry bar, removed the plate, and tore out the wiring. The light went out in the top of the elevator, and the doors stopped trying to close. We were four minutes behind schedule.

16

I WAS MOVING down one side of the ballroom heading for the back wall when I saw her. She had both hands on the armrests of a wheelchair, and lots of jewelry adorned those hands. Her face had no expression, none at all, and it was hard to imagine it ever having one. It looked like a face I had seen one time in a museum — a stone face that didn't move, black eyes in a pale, round, white stone face, the eyes too dark to see into. She wasn't exactly fat, just sort of round and compact, sitting there in the wheelchair without moving, watching Fontana up on the stage. Two men were seated on her right, and a third, smaller guy on her left. The smaller guy wasn't actually small, just in comparison to the other two. All three had mustaches, like Menoyo had said, and good haircuts and suits. The two on her right folded their arms and sat up straight in their chairs.

"Damas y caballeros," Fontana said, the microphone squealing. "Ladies and gentlemen. Please do not be alarmed, and please remain in your seats. Your ship has been temporarily appropriated by members of " — here he paused, and a flourish came from the drummer nearby — "the October Twenty-eighth Brigade!"

Behind Fontana, Krystal was struggling with the big Cuban flag I had seen in the mini-warehouse in Miami draped over the Dumpster. She had fastened one corner to the wall, and now she was on her tiptoes smacking a nail with a shoe borrowed from the bandleader. The bandleader sat on a folding chair watching her, massaging his foot. The musicians had put down their instruments.

"What is the October Twenty-eighth Brigade? What is our purpose? It is this: to correct an egregious error that has occurred in recent times at the highest levels of our government, the government of the United States. Behind me is the flag of our beloved Cuba. We are common men and women who love America but also love our first homeland and who have made every effort at dialogue before taking up arms in our struggle. What struggle is this? It is a struggle for freedom — not for ourselves but for our countrymen, who lie imprisoned by a rapacious tyrant."

With that a titter of applause came from the tables in the ballroom, something I hadn't expected. I was moving back and forth along the back wall, trying to watch people's hands. Miriam Benages wasn't one of the ones clapping. Her hands stayed on the armrests of her wheelchair.

Bryant was on one side of the stage, Kip on the other, standing in front of the double doors of the ballroom. Candle lanterns twinkled on each table, even the ones where no one was sitting. It made for poor light. Everyone but Fontana had his rifle ready.

"*¡Viva Cuba!*" Fontana yelled into the mike, too loud. Another titter of applause.

"Soon we will leave you," he went on. "It will be up to your captain to decide whether you continue on your voyage to Havana. But I beg you: if and when you reach that haunted shore, do not leave this ship. Do not set foot on Cuban soil until justice has been returned to that island and the tyrant cast out. Do not spend your hard-earned dollars in that city, for those dollars only serve to shore up the devil in his fortress. And when you return to your home, join us in your own small way, in spirit and in action. Write to your elected officials; explain to your neighbors; do not be fooled by this outrageous turn toward appeasement —"

"Fontana!"

He had paused to catch his breath, and in that pause she had raised her arm and leaned forward in her wheelchair. At the end of her arm, her hand held out a finger, pointed at him.

"Jack Fontana!"

It would have been a scream, but it was too even, too controlled, and too clear.

Fontana's face was invisible behind the mask.

Then he was trying to unsling the gun from his shoulder. My eyes went back to her in time to catch her turning away from having said something to the man on her left. The man was coming into a crouch, knocking his leg against the table as he came up. He fired before I could swing the rifle toward him, my middle finger on the trigger.

He was after Fontana, but the shot hit Krystal in the throat. She stumbled backward, falling against the flag, trying to find where she was hit, going onto her knees. I put two rounds in the shooter, and he sat down in his chair, knocking over the candle lantern.

A few people had dived to the floor, but most hadn't. Fontana was already off the stage and moving toward the table, Bryant coming in to flank him, stumbling once when he stepped on somebody. People were screaming. Kip had leaped onto the stage. He had grabbed Krystal in his arms and was starting toward the double doors that led out of the ballroom.

One of the two big guys managed to get off a round before Fontana shot him. The third man hadn't moved. Bryant came in beside Fontana, point-blank range across the table, and shot the third man in the chest.

I watched Fontana put the muzzle of his rifle against the woman's forehead and hold it there. I was coming up the side of the ballroom very fast now, scanning behind me and in front of me, sweeping the room. When I was close I could see that she was spattered with blood. The guy I had shot slumped a little and rolled off his chair onto the floor, leaving a chrome-plated pistol on the table.

All at once the woman's head jerked forward, and Fontana flinched. She had spat on him, a good one too, catching him full on the mask. He lowered his rifle. Bryant and I kept covering her.

Fontana started laughing. He sat down in the chair across from her, really giggling now. Finally he stopped. Bryant's hands were shaking. Kip was standing at the front of the room next to the doorway with Krystal in his arms.

Fontana had brought the cordless microphone with

him from the stage. He pulled it out of his pocket and spoke into it. "Ladies and gentlemen, we will leave you now. For your safety, please remain here until — until you are instructed to do otherwise."

He dropped the microphone on the table and lowered his voice, still looking at the woman. Then he said: "How many Cubans does it take to screw in a light-bulb?"

The woman, Miriam Benages, kept looking at him.

"Señora?" He leaned toward her. She didn't say anything.

"One brigade," Fontana said, sitting back in the chair, gazing at her. "With artillery and air support from the U.S. Navy."

He got up. We moved backward quickly, watching the room as we went, and passed through the doorway on the side of the stage and into the stairwell. On one of the landings we passed the little black man in tan coveralls who had been sitting on the bunk in the holding cell where we'd put the officers. He stood on the landing, holding his prayer book in one hand as we passed by.

17

KRYSTAL WAS DEAD. I stood in the cargo doorway and helped Bryant hand her down to Kip. He dragged her to the stern of the lobster boat and then carried her inside the little cabin.

Fontana sat on one of the stainless-steel prep counters. Krystal's needlepoint lay beside him, the ducks and kittens speckled with blood and all but finished. He poured a glass of mineral water and shook a couple of pills out of his pill bottle.

"Where's Menoyo?" I said.

"Cuffed in the cooler."

"How did she recognize you?"

He laughed. "I must have left an indelible impression the last time we met." He stood up suddenly and turned around and slapped himself on both buttocks. "Bang!" he yelled, springing forward in the air, his toes pointed at the floor. He landed in a crouch, wiggled once, then straightened and turned to face me, spreading his arms wide. "Hard to forget someone who shot you in the ass, wouldn't you say? Or the pelvis, correctly speaking. As it happens, I'm the reason Miriam's been sitting in a wheelchair for nine years."

The Dumpster was closed up and ready to go. Bryant had attached the hoist chain, and now he was down on the stern of the lobster boat, checking where the Dumpster would go. Kip was sitting on the gunwale, not saying or doing anything.

"Take those extra boxes and burn them," Fontana said. "The incinerator's that way."

"They wouldn't fit in the Dumpster?"

"No, Matthew, they wouldn't fit in the Dumpster. Come on, we're wasting time."

There were five of the powdered-milk cartons, each one about the size of a liquor box. I put my gun on the counter and pushed the pallet jack down the galley and got through the doors and stopped to look back. Fontana was taking up the slack in the hoist chain, and I waited to see the Dumpster swing free of the floor and hang in the air. While I was watching I saw the open door of a little office, the chef's office. Just inside the door, on the desk, were several bottles of wine, different kinds. I grabbed one and put it with the boxes on the pallet. Then I went down the corridor.

The incinerator was inside an alcove room littered with cardboard scraps. I pushed the mask up on my head, opened the incinerator doors, and saw how to switch the thing on. Then I sat on the powdered milk boxes and wondered how I would open the wine. I had a folding knife, but the blade was too wide to shove the cork down into the bottle. While I was thinking about just breaking the neck, I saw a little steel stem sticking out from the handle of the pallet jack. I held the bottle sideways against the stem and shoved, and the cork went in, squirting red wine on my hand. I turned the bottle up and took a big drink and then put it down on the floor while I loaded the boxes into the incinerator and watched them start to burn.

I had another couple of swallows and went out in the corridor, leaving the pallet jack but taking the bottle. The label on the bottle was a drawing of a house, a big estate with vineyards planted all around it. It was a place I had actually been once in California with my wife. I paused outside the galley door and took another drink. I would have a couple more and put the bottle back in the chef's office on the way through the galley.

I opened the galley door as quietly as I could and at

the far end of the long room I saw a wheelchair and Miriam Benages's head, with her short black hair. I could see Fontana and Bryant standing in the cargo doorway, unarmed, the Dumpster hanging out over the side of the ship at the end of the hoist boom, rain blowing back through the doors.

I had stopped, but now I started moving again, thinking what a lucky break to have come in so quietly. It gave me a chance. There was no way to set the wine bottle down without making noise. When I was halfway across the galley she heard me and turned the wheelchair fast with her left hand so that it was sideways in the space between two prep counters. Fontana and Bryant froze.

It was a single-barrel shotgun, cut off short, and as soon as I saw her start to turn and bring the gun across her body I began to run. The blast must have hit a bunch of the pots hanging from racks overhead because after the blast, even half deaf, I could hear pots and pans clattering all over the place. She pumped the slide but didn't have time to aim. The second blast went even wider than the first.

I turned my ankle as I brought the bottle down on her head, and instead of her head, I hit her shoulder. A sound came out of her, a grunt. She still had the gun, but

I had it now, too, the barrel scalding my hand. I brought my arm up, and this time I smacked her hard on the side of the face with the bottle and pulled hard on the gun at the same time. It came out of her hands, and I fell back on the floor, the gun sliding out of sight under a counter. She was still struggling, scrambling and grabbing for something under the seat of her wheelchair, trying to get at whatever it was, and going *unh! unh!* as she did it. Bryant was moving now, but he slipped and fell hard when he hit a patch of Krystal's blood. I heard Kip outside yelling like crazy from the lobster boat.

What happened next happened so quickly it was like a dream. I was behind her, behind the wheelchair. I got it by both handles and ran with it, shoving it along in front of me. Then I let go. Miriam Benages went straight through the cargo doorway and the chair hit the side of the Dumpster that was hanging in the air outside. Then came a dull bang, maybe her hitting the lobster boat and then going into the water.

I walked back to the wine bottle. It wasn't broken, and some wine was still in it. I picked it up and killed it. Kip was really hollering now.

Bryant got up and went over to the cargo doorway. He crouched down and peered over the lower edge. Fontana hadn't moved.

"I can't see her," Bryant said. "Christ, Matt," he continued, starting to laugh. He took an orange life ring from a hook and tossed it through the doorway into the night.

"The blood," Fontana said. "We need to hose down all this blood. Then we're ready to go."

18

I KEPT EXPECTING something to go wrong with the hoist, but it didn't. We got the Dumpster in place on the lobster boat, chained it down, and that was that. Kip cast off the mooring line, and we were free.

I watched the *Empress* drop away behind us until she no longer blazed but just twinkled in the distance. Then she was only a light, and after a long time she was gone.

It was nearly one a.m. I scanned the horizon with binoculars, but there was nothing to see. Or not yet, anyway. Inside me, like looking down a tube, I saw a piece of what I knew was out there, coming toward us. I saw a steep hull cutting black water, the hull painted with numbers, dim in the darkness but done up in the bright colors of the Coast Guard that would be strong and bold in sunlight.

For twenty minutes we motored up and down the long, rolling swells with the running lights dark. We had to take it slow with the Dumpster on board. Bryant was under the cabin roof, steering, while Fontana studied the radar screen and fiddled with the GPS. A sliver of moon came out from behind a cloud, and then the engines went to idle and we stopped moving. Bryant got on top of the cabin roof with a flashlight and blinked it, and pretty soon I could see a light coming at us dead ahead.

Julia was on the bow of the *Ya-Ya* with a line in her hands, and when the cabin cruiser got in close, she threw the line to Bryant. He tied it off to our bow, giving it plenty of slack. I watched Manny climb into the spotting tower and back the *Ya-Ya* down and cut the engines.

Fontana cursed and came out of the cabin, brushing past me. I ducked inside and looked at the radar. A pair of green dots had appeared on the edge of the screen, thirty miles to the north.

It took all four of us to get the cement block over the side, the thing that would anchor the Dumpster. It must have weighed three hundred pounds, with a big metal ring in the center. Before we started lifting, Bryant clipped the end of a cable onto the ring. Then the cement block went in with a splash, and the cable started running off a big spool mounted on the back of the lobster boat. When the cable was two-thirds gone, Fontana tested the hand brake and then let the rest of the cable unspool until only a few wraps were left. He applied the brake until the cable stopped paying out. Now the cement block hung a thousand feet beneath us.

Kip hauled on the chain hoist until the Dumpster came off the deck and kept coming, a few inches above the low gunwales in the stern. Everyone but Kip moved to one side of the boat, and then Kip swung the boom over the other side. The boat tilted sideways, but not as much as I had guessed it would. Kip went back to the chain hoist, clicked a switch, and started hauling on it again. The Dumpster came down from the boom, settling into the water, and the boat rose back to level.

The Dumpster floated beside the lobster boat, tethered to it with a line, with most of its bulk beneath the water.

Kip disappeared over the side with a mask and flippers and a flashlight. Bryant handed him one end of a chain. Next I saw light moving under the Dumpster. Then Kip was coming back on board, throwing the flashlight over first.

"All set?" Fontana asked.

"Yeah."

Using the hand brake to keep the spool from spinning too fast, Fontana let out almost all the rest of the cable. There was a loop in the cable nearly at the end of the spool. Fontana stopped the cable playing out, and Bryant attached the end of the chain to the loop.

"Untie it," Fontana said. "Quickly."

Kip took the line off the cleat and threw it across the Dumpster. Then he shoved until the Dumpster moved a few feet away from the side of the lobster boat.

Bryant went under the cabin roof and got the bolt cutters and came back out, ready to cut the cable from the spool.

"OK," Fontana said.

Bryant cut the cable. The chain pulled tight and slipped over the corner of the transom. When I looked, coming out of the cabin with two gallon cans of diesel fuel in my hands, the Dumpster was already gone, leaving a puff of foam and bubbles where it had been. Fontana was at the controls in the cabin, writing something on a scrap of paper.

We followed the *Ya-Ya* north for what I guessed was ten minutes. Bryant steered the lobster boat while Fontana stood beside him. He was holding the scrap of paper in his hand, looking at it from time to time. He would look at it, then close his eyes, moving his lips. He walked back to the stern and handed me the paper.

"Memorize it," he said.

It was the coordinates for the Dumpster, a string of numbers to mark the location. "What if I just hold onto this?" I asked.

"Don't be ridiculous," he said.

The two boats came together. Julia threw down a pair of canvas bags, and we all stripped and changed clothes, leaving our old ones in a pile on the lobster boat with everything else: masks, guns, body armor, gloves. Fontana and Bryant went through the cabin cruiser and brought two more pistols and some charts onto the lobster boat. Then everyone but Kip got back on board the *Ya-Ya*.

Before I went I looked at the radar and felt my mouth go dry. The green dots had moved closer together and much closer to the center of the screen: sixteen miles.

From the *Ya-Ya* I watched Kip go inside the cabin on the lobster boat and bend down where Krystal was. He was out of sight for about a minute. Then he appeared in the doorway and poured the two cans of diesel fuel over the decks, into the cabin, and all over the stern. He dipped his hands over the side, scrubbed them, and climbed into the *Ya-Ya*'s stern. Manny gunned the engines and got us a hundred feet out.

The next thing was something different. Fontana came out of the salon with an object I hadn't seen before on the cabin cruiser: a bow, with a quiver of target arrows clipped to its side. It was a complicated-looking rig, all wires and pulleys and sights, something a tournament archer would use. He handed the bow to Julia.

She nocked an arrow against a dot on the bowstring. While she stood at full draw, Fontana used tape to fasten a wad of cloth near the tip of the arrow. He lit it with a cigarette lighter and stood back, and suddenly the arrow vanished with a *slap-crack* of the bowstring, gone across the water like tracer fire. I looked and saw it lodged in the transom of the lobster boat, still aflame.

The fire went quickly up the stern and into the cabin. Then it really started burning.

Kip sat on one of the deck chairs and watched the fire fall away behind the *Ya-Ya*. He had taken something out of a handkerchief and started eating it. I stood beside him and looked at the fire, barely more than a light in the darkness now, far away and starting to disappear between swells. You could hear the *pop-pop* of ammunition going off. What Kip was eating was pale, with blood on it, a piece of raw meat. He put the last bite in his mouth and chewed, looking at the firelight, then got up and washed his hands over the side.

Julia came up behind me, kissed the back of my neck, and put a glass in my hand. I took a drink and smiled at her and then went to help Bryant start baiting hooks and putting them over the sides on outriggers. In a few more minutes Manny cut back to trolling speed, and we started fishing along a weed line.

We got strikes almost right off the bat, and by the time the first Coast Guard boat showed up, we had one cooler nearly full of dolphin fillets.

PART THREE

SNOW

19

THE NEXT FEW HOURS were like something coming slowly but definitely to a stop, decelerating in Key West and ending all at once in Miami.

The revenue cutter *Diligence* stood off from the *Ya-Ya* for thirty minutes while we sat on the stern in the glare of a big spotlight. At one point Manny tried to go down to the head but a loudspeaker crackled and a voice told him to stay where he could be seen and to keep his hands in plain view. The voice was polite and calm, but whoever was on the bridge of the Coast Guard boat seemed to be having trouble deciding what to do, or maybe he was waiting for orders from shore. After a few minutes Manny stood up and took a leak over the side, face to face with the kid in the orange life vest who was trying to look fierce behind the big swivel gun mounted on the cutter's bow.

At last they boarded us. I thought they would search the boat, tear into it with rams and crowbars, but I was wrong. One guy checked the engine room and the forward areas and got ready to take over the controls.

We were ordered aboard the cutter. An officer asked Fontana questions about where we had been and where we were going. Then they split us up and put us in separate cabins, and there was nothing more until we pulled into Key West.

I lay on a cot and listened to the engine drone coming through the walls. The cabin was white and blank, and I guessed it was just below the waterline. It was so clean and empty that I couldn't tell if I had dozed off or not when the engine sound changed, and there were voices and footsteps and a gentle bumping of the hull.

I must have been the last one they came for. When the two men in suits took me up onto the deck in handcuffs and down the gangway to the waiting car, there was no sign of Julia, Kip, Fontana, Manny, or Bryant.

The driver lit a cigarette and rolled down the window, and I watched the old wooden houses of Key West pass by. It wasn't far to the jail, and pretty soon I figured out they were winding around town, taking a ride.

The driver asked me about the cut over my eye. It was the damnedest thing, I told him. I was leaning over the side of the boat untangling a line when a barracuda jumped out of the water and smacked me in the head.

Could get infected, he said. But it looks like someone had the sense to sterilize it before they did a nice job sewing it up.

Julia, I explained. Julia Bonnell. I think she's a nurse.

Think? said the guy in the passenger seat, turning to look over his shoulder. I go fishing with people, I usually want to know 'em pretty well. You could get in trouble otherwise, going off with a bunch of strangers on a boat. You could get mixed up in something you didn't really mean to be mixed in with. Something that seemed like sort of a joke at first and then got serious, landed you in a heap of shit. Where's she from, you maybe know that?

You'd have to ask her, I responded.

He laughed and said: We will. I guarantee you we will.

"Take a look," said the guy in the passenger seat, opening a file folder and raising a sheaf of fax paper for the driver to see. A photo of Julia caught my eye. She stood in profile holding a bow. Other archers were in the background, all women.

"*Southeastern Regional Collegiate Champion,*" said the driver, reading the photo caption.

The other one nodded, putting the newspaper clipping back in the folder. "She went to school with Mike's kid. Sweet piece of ass, huh?"

The two of them then, pretending I wasn't in the backseat anymore, the guy with the cigarette talking about me: He was one of us, you know that? The other playing dumb, saying, Yeah? Yeah, the driver said. You know what they called him in the Miami field office? Loose Cannon Shannon. The one looking over his shoulder again, saying, Hey. Why'd they call you that, anyway? Mr. Shannon? Loose Cannon Shannon?

I can't remember, I said, and I didn't say anything else after that. We drove on, getting to the jail with the sun coming up.

I figured I would see the magistrate in the early afternoon, but I was wrong on that one, too. Breakfast was red Kool-Aid and corned beef hash, and the hash was good. A wino was lying on the floor of the holding cell, shaking and moaning. One of the black guys across the cell gave me a glance, and I knew we were thinking the same thing, and pretty soon we split up the wino's hash and ate it. There was nowhere to lie down except the floor, and I was about to do it, but the door opened, and then I was walking down the corridor and out through the sally port in an orange jumpsuit that was about two sizes too small.

A pair of marshals stood next to a prisoner van that

had exhaust smoke coming out the tailpipe in the cold morning air. A street sweeper passed by, and I could smell garbage and rotting flowers from a nearby alley, the old, low-tide smell of morning in Key West. The marshals handcuffed my hands in front and attached the cuffs to a waist chain and put on leg irons. Then they put me in the van, which was about half full. Fontana, Kip, and Bryant were all in there, sitting toward the back with the rest of the prisoners, mostly young black guys and beat-up, middle-aged white men with leathery skin and long, stringy hair. We went north, and I watched the sights along the Overseas Highway until Key Largo, where I wet my pants, unable to hold it any longer. More towns and places passed by: Homestead, Naranja, Goulds, all the old whistle-stops along the railroad line that had been taken up years ago. And then we were pulling into the new federal building in downtown Miami, pausing at a guardhouse. There were steel barriers, like teeth, in the down-sloping driveway, designed to protect the building from car bombers. The barricades retracted, flattening slowly into the pavement. We drove into the basement, got loaded onto an elevator, and were marched across a skyway into the jail on the other side of the street. After the strip search I got a new jumpsuit and a private eight-by-ten cell where the lights never went off and I was tired enough not to care.

20

THE DOOR of the conference room swung open. A man with a briefcase stepped inside and the trusty went back out and locked the door behind him.

The briefcase was black, and not one of these fashionable wafers. It was big and heavy-looking: a briefcase that had some real work going on inside it, that got opened and closed a lot in the course of any day.

The man wore a tan suit and a tropical tie. He was in his late forties or early fifties, with skin that looked embalmed.

"Good afternoon, Mr. Shannon," he said. "My name is Carl Sandolin. I'm your lawyer."

"I didn't hire a lawyer."

"No," he replied. "That's true."

He clicked open the briefcase and took out two airline bottles of Scotch. Then he shut the briefcase quickly, as though something might escape if he left it open very long. The bottles didn't clink when he held them because they were made of plastic. He set them down in the middle of the table.

"You can, of course, decline the legal counsel I've been hired to provide you," he said.

I looked at him while I reached out for one of the bottles. I could feel my hand shaking.

"Sleeping OK?" he asked.

"Like a baby."

He didn't seem to be in a hurry. He sat down across the table from me while I finished the first Scotch and started on the second. He frowned to himself, looking out into space, and began rummaging in his coat pockets. He kept frowning and tried his pants pockets. While he was stirring around I noticed he was wearing suspenders. The suspenders had little dollar signs all up and down them.

"Well," he said, "the United States Attorney for the Southern District of Florida has got it in his head that you helped hijack a cruise ship, murder three DEA agents, and steal a bunch of money that belongs to a drug baron." He coughed. "Or baroness." He had found what he was after in his pants pocket, and now he was taking a cough drop out of a yellow paper package. "That's a problem."

He sucked on the cough drop for a while. "Fisherman's Friend," he said, handing over the package. "If you've never had one, you're in for a treat. This is the aniseed version. There's the original variety, too, and they're even stronger, which you'll find hard to believe."

I took one out and put it in my mouth. The cough drop had a good, strong licorice flavor that went nicely with the aftertaste of the Scotch.

He settled back in the chair. "On the bright side, the feds don't seem to have any evidence. Except, of course, circumstantial evidence. They think it's a wee bit suspicious that the security director for a cruise line should be discovered floating around on Halloween night in international waters a stone's throw from the site of a cruise ship hijacking. But we'll deal with that later. Meanwhile I'm going to get you out of here on probably two hundred thousand dollars' bond."

He was watching me a bit more carefully now. "The same goes for Miss Bonnell. I've already met with her, briefly. She seems just fine."

"What about Fontana?"

"Mr. Fontana has been questioned and transferred to Mount Sinai, where there's an FBI agent sitting by his bedside. Mr. Purvis and Mr. Rodríguez Colón have already bonded out. Mr. Bryant may be lingering in the federal system for some time. He's being asked about an armored-car holdup in Tacoma from nineteen ninety-two and another the following year, in Fresno.

"Now," he continued. "Let's make sure we have our facts straight. You got off work on Friday, drove to Key West, and went fishing with your stepbrother, Jack Fontana, and some friends. You thought it might be the last time you would have a chance to go fishing with Mr. Fontana because of his illness. Mr. Fontana brought along a lady friend, Miss Bonnell, a registered nurse from Minneapolis vacationing in sunny Florida. You invited your old army cohort, Kip Purvis, and he in turn brought an acquaintance, Bobby Bryant, whose alleged felonious adventures in the past you knew nothing about. A good time was had by all, except that Mr. Fontana got sick, so you started back to Key West early. You don't know a thing about the October Twenty-eighth Brigade or the hijacking of the *Norwegian Empress* except what you've seen on TV or heard secondhand."

"No," I agreed. "I don't."

"The only thing you can figure out is that this is some sort of bizarre stratagem to get you fired from your job as security director for Festival Cruises."

"Yes," I said. "That's right."

He laughed. He laughed so hard he started coughing,

but the whole time he was laughing and coughing his skin stayed the same color. Then he stopped laughing and sat there, looking at me.

"Any questions, then?"

"Yeah. A minute ago you said something about three DEA agents. About them being murdered."

"Correct. Three DEA agents were shot and killed in a fracas that took place in the ballroom aboard the *Norwegian Empress* at some point during the hijacking. They were part of a security detail assigned to protect a government witness who had agreed to testify against members of her own criminal organization. I'm referring to the lady cocaine kingpin from whom you purportedly helped steal thirty million dollars." He scratched the side of his nose and frowned. "Or should I say *queenpin*? You see, Mr. Shannon, this drug baroness and those three DEA agents were on their way to a rendezvous in the Cayman Islands, where she had pledged to identify a high-level Colombian drug supplier and otherwise assist the DEA in arresting him, by acting as lure. Whoever hijacked the *Norwegian Empress* seems to have inadvertently interrupted a rather complicated and sensitive undercover sting operation. More questions?"

"How do you know all this?"

He smiled. "I read several newspapers each and every morning."

He kept smiling and raised his eyebrows.

I shook my head.

"Fine," he said. "I guess that's it, then. If there's any talking to be done, let me do it, please. Don't volunteer anything." He put a white card on the white table. "I want you to contact me as soon as you're released."

He sat there for another few moments waiting to see if I would say anything. Then he stood up and knocked for the trusty.

"I've enjoyed our time together," he said. "Would you like another cough drop?"

"No."

"Again, Mr. Shannon, you do want to call. You want to hang on to my business card almost as though your life depended on it. Will you?"

"Sure. I'll keep it right with me."

There was no way in hell I was walking out of there on a $200,000 bond, or any other bond. But the next morning, around ten thirty, I did.

21

T HEY LET ME OUT the same way they had brought
me in, through the sally port behind the new federal building. I walked three blocks to the south and
then a couple more to the west, watching the birds cir-
cling the top of the old courthouse on Flagler Street. I
stopped to look in a window full of cheap electronics
and glanced back down the street. Two-car surveillance
is what I would have used, with at least one agent on
foot because it was so congested down here on Monday
mornings.

I spotted a Jeep Cherokee with tinted windows and
the right kind of antenna and wondered if it was someone's idea of a joke: I had checked the same vehicle out
of the motor pool about four years ago for a job. A young

guy was window-shopping across the street. He had been with me, about two hundred feet back, ever since I walked out of the jail. I couldn't see a second car.

I went up Flagler Street and into Sally Russell's and sat down at the bar. It was dark inside and bright on the street, and even though it was early for lunch, people were coming into the restaurant. Every time someone came in, I could see out the door. The window-shopper came by, looked at the door, and kept moving. He reappeared across the street and bought a hot dog from a vendor. He stood there and looked at it for a while before he ate it.

I ordered a drink and waited. The traffic on Flagler was creeping along. I put the glass down on the bar and watched the nose of a Mercedes edge into the slot view I had onto the street. Then the door closed. When it opened again the Mercedes was still there, broadside to the doorway so that I could see both its front and rear windows. The front window was lowered, and I saw the lawyer, Carl Sandolin, sitting in the driver's seat. The rear window started rolling down just as the door of the restaurant closed. I waited again. A fat man in a suit came through the door. When he had walked past me I looked out into the street. Right there at the curb the Mercedes had its rear window rolled all the way down. The woman's face, the face of Miriam Benages, was turned straight at me. She took off her sunglasses and kept staring, her eyes looking into mine. Then she put the glasses back on. The window started rolling up, and the door onto the street closed. As soon as it did, I started for the back of the restaurant.

The bathroom was a fancy one, three stalls and urinals, a big mirror and sinks along one wall. An old black guy was sitting on a stool reading a newspaper. He watched me in the mirror while I went into a stall and locked the door. I knew what I was going to do but I wanted to think about it for another minute. After I did I flushed the toilet, came out of the stall, and went over to the sink like I was going to wash my hands. The guy on the stool looked at me, and I looked at him. Then I dropped my eyes and bent over the sink.

As long as you look at someone they stay alert and can sense what you're going to do next. But now I was looking down, reaching for the faucet, and scanning the bottles and cans the washroom attendant had spread out in front of the mirror beside a stack of hand towels and a tip basket — aftershave and cologne, talcum powder, breath mints, Grecian Formula hair tonic.

I came up fast and hit him. The punch was off a little, almost as though he'd moved. Then my left ear exploded. Just as quick I felt the breath go out of my body from where he had hit me in the rib cage. I was so surprised I almost went down. In fact, I had started to. I used that place, that sort of crouch, to come up from with an uppercut. But he had moved, stepping toward the door. I tried to get in close, but he circled past the front of a stall and got his back around by the sink.

I noticed two things then, in that special way you notice things right before you realize you're probably going to get your clock cleaned. The first was the chain around his neck with a cross pendant. It wasn't a necklace at all. It was a tattoo, the whole thing — cross, chain links, and all — done in prison-yard blue. The second thing was a clutter of shiny little trophies way over on the left near his tip basket. The trophies had figures of boxers on the tops of them.

I tried a jab, but he slapped it away. He said, "Guess someone woke up on the wrong side of bed." I kept my hands up close to my head, waiting for an opening. I faked with a right and tried to tag him with another jab, but he moved again. "Guess you got some reason for tryin' to whip a old man's ass," he said, keeping his feet busy. "A old man never did you no harm." Then he said, "Stop fightin' me for a minute."

There was nowhere for him to back off to, so I stepped back good and far, back toward the door. He put his hands down in front of him. I did the same, chest level anyway, not taking any chances.

"What you want?" he said. "You want money, I ain't givin' it. That's all I got." He meant the tip basket. There was a dollar bill and some coins in it. "I put the dollar in there myself, make it look like some big spender come through." He looked me up and down, looked at my shoes. "You don't need money," he said. "Someone after you?"

"Several someones," I said.

He nodded. "What you want?"

"To look different," I said.

"Different clothes," he said, nodding. "Different hair, maybe. Walk right outta here. They gone try to hurt me if I help you?"

"They might."

"Good. Helpin' someone don't count if it don't cost you nothin'."

I didn't know what to say. "I guess you did some boxing."

"I done all kinds of foolish shit before I found my personal Savior," he said. "Look. Calm down and go in there and take your clothes off. I'm goin' to help you. Why you didn't just ask me in the first place?"

I went in the stall and took off my shoes and got undressed. Someone came in and took a leak at the urinal, washed his hands, and went back out. I passed my pants over the door, and the old man passed his back. I put them on. They were almost a perfect fit. He handed me his shirt, and I put that on.

"You want your belt?" he said.

"No, you keep it."

"It's a nice one. Thank you."

I put my own shoes on my feet and came out of the stall. He handed me a razor, and I soaped up and started shaving.

"This ain't goin' to smell too good, but it might do the trick." He was holding a can of white shoe polish. He dipped some out and mixed it with a smaller amount of black from another can and went to work on my hair, making it gray.

A little pillow lay on the stool where he waited for customers. He picked it up and pointed to the stall.

"Take the laces out your shoes," he said.

I did and then unbuttoned my new shirt. He tied the pillow so that when I buttoned up the shirt I had grown a paunch.

"That cane, I just keep it for company. I don't need it, so you take it."

He watched me walk with the cane, and then he took it and walked with it, showing me how.

"Listen," he said. "They had me in a box once, just

like you in a box now. It took me a long time to figure my way out of it. You know what I figured out? There wasn't any box. Just the box I made for myself. I'll bet the box you in now got to do with money. Money or pussy. Or money *and* pussy. You get out of your box and you still got your hands on some money, you send me a little piece of it."

He handed the cane back. "Every crutch is a weapon," he said. "You think about that, maybe figure out what I mean. Do your ribs hurt?"

"Yes, they do."

He laughed. "That way you remember me. Good luck."

I went out past the bar and into the street and up Flagler toward the bay, taking it slow and limping up a storm. When I got to the Seybold Building I crossed the street and walked inside and kept going past all the jewelry shops until I came out the other side of the arcade onto First Street. I waited until I saw a cab, flagged it down, and told the driver to head for the airport.

I walked up four levels of ramps in the long-term parking garage before I found what I was after. I'd been hoping for a delivery truck, but this was even better: a big V-8 Buick with New York plates and a U-Haul trailer hitched to the back. I could see the parking receipt tucked in a slot on the dashboard. The inside of the car was clean and tidy. It belonged to someone older, someone careful, and that told me something.

It took me less than a minute to find the magnetic hide-a-key under the front bumper.

22

THE MEETING PLACE was the corner of Fifth and Ocean, every day at noon. I came over the causeway, crossed Washington, and started paying attention. At the corner I kept looking until the light changed, then circled the block to make another pass. I was five minutes early. A girl on Rollerblades got up from a bench across the street and skated diagonally right through the intersection. She was ten feet away before I realized it was Julia. She got in the car, taking a pair of binoculars from around her neck. The light changed.

"I almost didn't recognize you," she said. "You look ridiculous."

"So do you."

She laughed, and I laughed.

"Any sign of the others?"

"No, none," she said, unlacing the Rollerblades. "When did they let you out?"

"About ten thirty this morning. I'm going to circle around once or twice more."

I did. No Kip, no Manny.

"Fontana's in the hospital," I said.

"I know. I went to see him this morning after I got out."

"And?"

"Well, he's plenty sick."

We crossed the bay, and I got on the expressway. Then I turned off onto U.S. 1, heading south. When we were passing the Dixie Creme, she said, "You're going to the warehouse. To get a gun?"

"Yes."

Ten minutes later I pulled off the highway and stopped the car at the end of the broad alley, looking down it at the door of the shop space. The alley was empty. I parked two spaces down from the door.

"I'm going in with you," she said. "There's something I want, too."

"I'll get it for you."

"You don't know where it is."

Before picking up Julia I had stopped at a hardware store and bought a pair of bolt cutters, and now I got them out of the trunk. She kept an eye on the alley while

I bent down and set the blades on the loop of the padlock and cut it. The lock dropped onto the concrete, and I thought I heard something from inside. I listened, trying to count up to twenty. I got to twelve and didn't want to keep standing in the alley holding a pair of bolt cutters.

She looked at me.

"I thought I heard something," I said.

She listened. Then she bent down, grabbing the door handle. I felt like telling her to wait, but the door was already running up on its slides.

She stepped inside and turned on the lights. As she was reaching for the switch, the smell hit me. It was something acrid and strong mixed up with the cement dust and epoxy odor and another new smell of fresh sawdust. The lights came on and she screamed and turned the lights off. In the darkness there was a voice from the back of the room. It was trying to shout, but it wasn't a shout. It was more of a croak. The voice had said: *"Under the water! It's under the water!"*

I didn't think I had really seen what I thought I had. I bumped her getting to the light switch, and she jumped and screamed again, even louder. When she screamed, I yelled. Then I turned on the lights and looked into the shop space, all the way to the back of the long room.

There were three wooden crosses about twelve feet high. A man was hanging from the one on the left, naked. Another man, skinnier and also naked, was hanging from the one on the right. The cross in the middle was empty, but the fresh lumber was flecked with blood. The man on the left moved his head, the muscles and tendons in his neck straining. *"Under the water!"* he croaked.

It was Kip. The man on the right must have been Manny. He hadn't moved.

I reached out and got hold of Julia's shoulder, but she pushed my hand away. I made myself turn around and roll down the door.

I walked in slowly. Julia stayed where she was.

The crosses were a neat job, two-by-ten floor joists put together with lag bolts. The empty one in the middle let me see how they were done. I noticed a little white card stapled to it about five feet off the ground, below where the horizontal and vertical joists came together. I took it down.

It was the lawyer's business card: Carl Sandolin, embossed, with a cell phone number, no address.

Kip was trying to yell again, but he choked. I looked at him. His eyes were half open but I could tell he couldn't see anything. Someone had driven galvanized sixty-penny nails neatly through both wrists, leaving about an inch of nail sticking out. The someone had wrapped fencing wire around each nail head and then around his wrists and around the joist. His feet hung down free against the cross. Shit was on his legs and on the cross and a little bit on the floor beneath both Kip and Manny. Manny seemed to be dead. His tongue was swollen and sticking out from between his teeth.

"It's under the water!" Kip whispered. When he spoke, his rib cage heaved up and down. I saw he was wearing a pair of headphones, taped in place. A wire ran down to a tape recorder fastened to the back of the cross. The tape inside it was turning.

I stood on a bait cooler and pulled the duct tape away from Kip's hair, keeping my eyes on him while I put the headset over my ears and listened. There was nothing at first. Then, after a few seconds, the voice of Miriam Benages said: *"Where — is — the money?"* I waited, and waited some more. Then she said it again, calmly: *"Where — is — the money?"* I listened to the question a third time, and it was exactly the same, no change in the way she said it. The entire tape was the one question, repeated over and over.

I jumped when I heard movement, but it was Julia crossing the room behind me. She went to a toolbox, opened it, and took the tray out. She dug around in the bottom and brought out a Gerber's baby-food bottle, unscrewing the lid. She dipped a key into the bottle and brought the key up to her face, held one side of her nose and sniffed, then dipped the key through the mouth of the bottle and brought it up to her face again, inhaling with the other side of her nose.

I couldn't figure out how to get him down from there. The cross was held up with chains hooked into the metal ceiling girders. The whole cross, with Kip on it, hung from the ceiling, swaying slightly. Kip didn't move or say anything, but I saw his eyes flicker. Something black was coming out the edge of his mouth and dripping down his chin.

The smell didn't seem so bad now. I picked up a handgun from the table and checked the action and the breach, popped out the clip. It was full. I kept the gun in my hand and looked at Julia. I found another gun and checked it and gave it to her.

We went out the door leaving the lights on, rolling the door back down.

● ● ●

THERE WAS A PHONE in the car. When we had turned onto the highway, I called 911 and gave the address of the warehouse and the shop-space number and hung up.

We turned west on Kendall and drove until we hit

Krome, then turned south. I pulled over and asked her for the baby-food jar and took a couple of key bumps, one for each nostril.

"I don't think we can do this by ourselves," I said.

She looked at me. Then she got out of the car and came around to my side. She opened the door.

"Get out," she said.

"No."

"Yes. Get out. If you want to quit, OK. But I'm not. I'm going all the way."

"Why?"

"Why? *Why?* Because it's dark inside a tobacco barn. Because I once ate nothing but kale and rotting pears for two straight weeks. Because the world is what it is, and people who allow themselves to become nothing don't have a place in it. That's why," she said.

"All right."

"All right what?

"We'll do it by ourselves. Together."

She looked at me steadily, then walked around to the passenger side and got back in.

We drove on for a time, and I asked her if she was OK.

"Yes."

"What are you thinking?"

"I'm thinking I never really thought about how you do it. I just assumed you put the nails through the palms. Not through the wrists. Not right between the radius and ulna."

I took my arm down off the seat and put both hands on the steering wheel, trying to think about the next move.

23

You keep looking at me," she said when she woke up between Homestead and Key Largo.

"You're nice to look at."

"That's not what I mean. You were already doing it in my room at the Cardozo the first time we talked."

I shrugged. "Some of the things you say. The way you say them. It reminds me of someone else."

"Who?"

"I don't know."

A car passed.

"Do you think we'll ever see him again?"

"Fontana?"

"Yes," she said.

"Sure. He's a survivor. So are you."

I looked over at her. She had her back against the door, watching me.

"Do you ever sit around and wonder about the child you and your wife gave up?"

"I don't know about the sitting around part, but yes, of course."

"But you never found out," she said.

"No. The law makes it pretty much impossible."

"A lot of those laws have changed."

"OK. But I'm not sure what the point would be. I guess I was never sure it was a good idea. I mean, look at you."

"What about me?"

"I thought you told me *you* were adopted. The music professor and his wife. It seems like they did fine by you."

"They did. But I wasn't adopted until I was thirteen."

"That sounds unusual."

"It is. My adoptive mother did volunteer work as a guardian ad litem. She got involved in my case, and they wound up taking me on full time, so to speak."

"Your case?"

"For the first thirteen years I was raised in a series of foster homes. Some were just OK. Some weren't. It appears I was a very clumsy child. I kept falling down and having to go to the hospital. The year before I was adopted I was living with a couple on a farm in North

Carolina. The husband and his brother liked to wake me up early and take me down to the tobacco barn for photo sessions. One of them would tie me up and fuck me while the other took pictures. Then they would trade off. Sometimes they would lock me up in the tobacco barn and leave me there all day. Until they came back at night. Have you ever been inside a tobacco barn, Matt? It's very dark, even in the day. It's hot. Snakes love it."

"Jesus."

"Yep."

"Then what happened?"

"A small-town scandal. They went to trial but in the end they were acquitted. They died earlier this month in a hunting accident."

"A hunting accident."

"Three days after Jack got out of prison."

I looked at her. "What are you telling me, Julia?"

She was silent.

"Are you telling me Jack had something to do with those men's deaths?"

"Toward the end, my foster father bought a movie camera, and a couple of years after the trial he started selling his film to an offshore Web site. It was a pioneer in live video streaming, primitive but popular. He made enough money to buy a new tractor."

She turned and looked at me. "Jack knew all about it. He helped shut down the Web site in ninety-four, when he was still working for the FBI. But he was never able to arrest the people behind it. Or at least not the main person. Miriam Benages."

I was glad to stop talking about it. It all left a bad set of images. But what had started us talking stayed put: something made me sure I had known her before, had met her, even though I knew I never had. She seemed to want to say something else, but she stopped talking when I turned off the highway onto the road leading up Big Pine Key. I was so tired I almost missed the turn, braking hard and throwing my arm out toward her the way my dad used to do with me. I had a plan now because I had remembered Dennis the Dentist.

The house stood on pilings all the way at the end of a sandy lane lined with empty lots. The dentist had built the house years ago, before the county put a moratorium on new construction and before he got caught trafficking Oxycontin and went to work for me as a government informant. He had planted all sorts of exotic trees, and now they had grown up and walled in the sandy yard. I could see a clue to what I was after over the crown of the roof — the top of a sailboat mast. I pulled in and kept going, getting around the back of the house to the canal where the sailboat lay roped to a faded dock.

The dentist came down from Miami on weekends, and the boat waited for him.

I backed the trailer up to the storage space under the house. We walked down to the dock and looked at the boat, a Morgan sloop, thirty-eight feet and plenty slow, but with lots of space inside. Julia went around to the stern and read the name, *Nellie,* and laughed.

We went up a staircase to the screened porch, and Julia flicked a button on the hot tub, and it started bubbling and rolling. The dentist had a collection of wind chimes on the porch, lots of them, and a big aquarium inside the house that I could see through the panes of the door. I took off my shirt and wrapped it around my arm and broke out one section of glass, then reached through and turned the handle. We went into the living room and sat down, looking at the aquarium.

● ● ●

IT WAS THE KIND OF PLACE I would have liked to have, and maybe someday I would. The dentist kept it neat as a pin. Lots of pictures of sea creatures decorated the walls, and a big piece of polished driftwood sat by the fireplace.

Julia walked across the living room, and I followed her. A door led into a little office and another opened into a bedroom. We stood in the doorway and looked at the bed. It was the biggest bed I had ever seen. On the table beside it was an expensive-looking sculpture of two men wrestling.

"This guy knows how to have fun," she said.

I wondered about that while I left her in the house to sweep up the glass and get some things together in the kitchen. The sun had gone down, but there was still light in the sky. I used the bolt cutters to open the trailer and used them again on the padlock on the hatch of the *Nellie*. Down inside the salon I found the panel box and flipped all the breakers. The engine key hung on a hook. I took it up into the cockpit and turned the engine over, letting it rumble while I checked the fuel and the running lights and the masthead light. The inside of the boat was like the inside of the house, clean and tidy. All the charts I needed were right there in a drawer beneath the navigation table. A teakettle waited on the gimballed stove in the galley, and a skinny little mock-Persian carpet was on the narrow cabin sole leading up to a V-berth in the bow. I shut down the engine and went to the car and got the guns and put one in the galley cabinet behind a coffee can and one in a compartment in the cockpit next to a winch handle. Then I went back to the trailer and started unloading. There were boxes of books and clothing and two bicycles; there was furniture, including a big armchair and a couch. I dragged the couch out last and got it into the storage space underneath the house.

When I went back up the steps Julia was in the hot tub, her hair spread out over the edge to stay dry. She dipped down when I came onto the screened porch. The baby-food jar sat on the corner of the tub. Under the moving water I could see the outline of her body. She laughed at me, her eyes sparkling, and I watched her as I kept moving across the deck through the door of the house and into the kitchen. Everything I had asked her to do was done. I carried a bag of food and two gallon jugs of drinking water onto the porch.

"When we're rich, I want to buy a place just like this," she said, pointing a toe at me from the water.

I almost stopped moving then but thought better of it. I would stop moving later, and for a long time.

I went down the stairs and put the things in the boat. I got in the car and worked it around so the trailer was ready and waiting to load when we came back. Then I got on board and started the engine, tested the roller furling on the jib, and removed the cover from the mainsail. We were ready to go. I looked up from the cockpit and saw her looking back at me from the screened porch, watching me watch her put her clothes on.

•　　•　　•

WE MOTORED TO THE END of the short canal and then across the backcountry water toward the bridge. Cars were coming over the causeway with their headlights on, and a couple of skiffs had anchored to do some night fishing there where the falling tide rushed past the bridge pylons. The top of the mast cleared the bridge with plenty of room to spare, and we kept going east through patch reefs and past little white floats that marked lobster traps, leaving the lights of the Overseas Highway behind us. When we got to Hawk Channel I pointed the boat into the wind and had Julia take the wheel while I went forward and raised the main. Then I came back to the cockpit and used the roller furling to get out the jib and turned southeast close-hauled, the boat heeling hard to starboard. I killed the engine, and we were airborne. Julia went below and made some coffee and brought it up, and after a time she went down to the salon and slept.

Later I would glance at the lighted compass in its binnacle and then look at her where she lay in the glow of the nav light. Key West was an hour behind us now. I watched her sleeping there inside where it was warm, and it made me feel warm. I wanted to take care of her, but I knew I was doing exactly the opposite, taking her toward something that could be serious trouble. I wondered if there was a way I could make a hiding place on the boat, a den like a fox would make to get down into and be safe. Maybe I could lock the wheel and go up to the V-berth and make a secret spot under the bunk, a space where she could hide if things went bad. But she had said she was afraid of the dark, of being closed up in a tight spot. The truth was I couldn't protect her. There wasn't any safety now. There was only the chance for it in the future.

But another part of me started to wonder: who was she, anyway? What did I really know about her? *Jack says you're a sucker for damsels in distress.* Maybe her latest story — the tobacco barn and the Web site — was just another tale, something to make me stick with her until she got the money. Thinking about the house on the island, the weekend home of Dennis the Dentist, made me realize I hadn't even thought what I might do with the money. I had been at the end of a life, a complete life that had run its course. It should have come to an end, but it hadn't. Lots of people were still walking around after their lives had stopped, ghosts really. The question was whether there was something beyond that, a way to start all over again. Could it be as simple as that, a snake shedding its skin or a fox turning a new color in the fall? I was going to find out. I was going to keep moving forward down the trail I was on, all the way to the end. She was part of it; but I also knew I was going to keep an eye on her once we had the money. I took the gun out of the little compartment near the winch handle and put it in my belt, there in the small of my back, good and close.

While I was thinking about all this, I was thinking about the coordinates, too. I was so tired I could barely see straight, but I had the pain in my ribs and the cold to keep me going. The coordinates would float in and out of my mind when I closed my eyes. I tried not to focus on them because I was afraid they would scatter and disappear. The problem was I had forgotten part of them, part of one string of numbers. I knew the way to bring the numbers back: it was like looking at something at dusk you can't quite make out. You look just to the side instead of straight on and then you catch a glimpse of it, the shape of whatever it is, in your peripheral vision. It was the same with the numbers. I closed my eyes, trying to relax and not think of anything, just feel the vibration of the rudder coming up through the rudder post and through the wheel into my hands. I would open my eyes a little and look at the lighted compass and then close my eyes again. A six and a one were moving around, revolving and floating in my mind. Then all at once the six and one stopped turning in the darkness, sort of glowing, and clicked into place. I could remember the whole sequence then, both strings: latitude and longitude, degrees, minutes, seconds; the seconds down to three decimal places. I could remember everything.

There was less heel to the boat ever since we had turned south at Key West, and less apparent wind. I locked the wheel and went down the stairs to the nav station and entered the coordinates in the GPS, figuring out how to set an alarm to tell me when we were getting close.

She woke up at sunrise. The wind had died almost to calm, and I started the engine. She helped me get the sails down and took the wheel while I lay on the quarter berth and slept until I heard the alarm going off.

I got the boat as close as I could to the spot, then kept it in place against the northbound Gulf Stream. The sea was nearly flat. After about forty minutes, when it was time, I started scanning for the Dumpster with binoculars. When it popped up and broke the surface, it was only sixty feet away.

24

SHE LEANED OVER to take the last box out of my hands. When I had climbed back on board, she put her arms around my neck and kissed me and then stepped away.

We stood in the cockpit looking at the empty Dumpster bobbing next to the sailboat, neither of us saying anything. The money was stacked inside the salon, the boat nearly full of boxes. I reached out to take her hand, but she was too far away and not reaching out. Then I heard what she heard: the high-pitched whine of an engine.

I stood on one of the cockpit seats. Just off to the left of the rising sun a rooster tail shot up from the back of a boat. The boat was coming at us fast, the engine already much louder. I got through the door and down the steps into the salon and grabbed the gun off the quarter berth where I had left it and fell going back up the stairs. Julia hadn't moved. She stood there with her mouth open, arms folded. The boat was fifty yards out and not slowing down.

I thought they would run right over us, but at the last moment the big Scarab throttled down, its bow plunging forward. I could see four men on board — one hanging out over each side with short rifles sighted on us, another driving, and one more behind the windscreen holding onto a grab rail. It was the last one who yelled at us as the boat turned broadside, idling, the rifles close in now.

"Mr. Shannon! Take that gun out of your waistband and pitch it in the water!"

I did. One of the two with rifles had come up onto the long, narrow bow of the Scarab and stepped catlike onto the sailboat. Then he was on one knee on the cabin roof, pointing his rifle at my chest. Julia started shaking, not looking at anything. I was keeping my hands out front where they could be seen. The second man kept his rifle on Julia and came aboard the way the first one had. So did Carl Sandolin.

He crawled and scooted his way past the two others until he got down into the stern of the sailboat and stood up. He was dressed in khakis and a green Polo shirt, and his skin was yellowish gray. He took a pistol out of a shoulder holster and hit me with it as hard as he could in the side of the head.

"You fuck!" he screamed. "Do you have any idea how much I hate boats?" Then he hit me again, and I was gone.

It must not have been for very long. When I came around I was sitting with my back against the transom. Sandolin was looking at me, sitting cross-legged on the cabin roof. The two others were moving the money as fast as they could. I looked down into the salon and saw they were almost done. One guy would pitch a box from the salon up into the cockpit. Another would pitch it from the sailboat cockpit into the Scarab. The man in the Scarab was heaving the boxes through a hatch into the speedboat's big bow compartment.

The guy in the salon moved to grab another box, and I saw Julia. She was on her knees up toward the V-berth, naked from the waist up. They had tied her hands behind her back and knotted a piece of cord around her neck. The other end of the cord was tied to the door of the lazarette in front of her, underneath the quarter berth. The cord made her lean forward. Her hair fell in her face. She wasn't making any sound, but I could see she was swaying back and forth and trembling.

Sandolin was sitting off at an angle so he could keep

his eyes on me, but the guy pitching boxes out of the cockpit kept getting between me and him. The lawyer was sucking on one of his cough drops while he looked at me and I looked back. He was shaking. While he sucked on the cough drop and looked at me, he kept clicking the rifle's safety. Off, on. Off, on. It was a nervous habit. He clicked the safety one way, and I saw the red pin pop out of the rifle bolt. He clicked it again, and the red vanished back inside the steel. On, off. On, off. He didn't know the gun well enough to know which position was on or off without looking. Sometimes he would glance down and look for the red to see that the safety was off. Then he would glance down again later and see what position it was in. I had to do something to make him stop looking at the safety.

There were a few more boxes in the salon, some piled on the table, but the man down there stopped and took a break while the guy in the cockpit hollered at the one in the Scarab. The guy in the Scarab had disappeared into the bow compartment, no doubt to rearrange boxes and make more space and settle the weight. I watched the man in the salon as he ran his hand through Julia's hair. He stepped over her and sat down on the quarter berth and grabbed the back of her head. He reached his hand down and started fondling one of her breasts. She didn't make any sound.

I decided to laugh.

Sandolin stared at me, sucking on his cough drop, clicking the safety. The guy in the cockpit glanced at me and then went back to waiting for the other guy to reappear from inside the Scarab's bow compartment. He lit a cigarette. The man in the salon had pulled Julia's head back and was kissing her on the lips. Now she was fighting him, trying to call out.

I laughed again like I had thought of the most amusing thing in the world.

"What's funny, Mr. Shannon?" Sandolin asked.

"You."

"Am I? Why is that?"

"Because I just thought of something I bet you're trying not to think about."

He sucked on the cough drop. "What would that be?"

"Steak," I said. "Steak and eggs. Eggs over easy, real runny, with hash browns and ketchup. Maybe a side of silver-dollar pancakes with maple syrup."

He didn't say anything. He looked sick. He spit the cough drop over the side and then spit saliva out of his mouth.

"In the old days, they had this cure for seasickness," I went on. "They would take a piece of whale blubber —"

Julia screamed, and the man slapped her and said something in Spanish. He stood up and unbuckled his pants. The one in the cockpit told the one in the Scarab to hurry up. He was finishing his cigarette.

"A piece of whale blubber about half the size of your fist," I said, "a good chunk, like a big piece of gray fat. They would tie a string around it. Then they would make the guy who was seasick swallow it."

Sandolin had stopped clicking the safety, and he wasn't looking down anymore. "Mr. Shannon —"

"When he had swallowed it, another guy would pull on the string, pull the chunk of whale blubber back out of his stomach and up his throat. Slowly."

It would take me two moves. One to get up, get my feet under me in a crouch; another to get to the guy with the cigarette. I wasn't sure how good my balance was going to be.

"Anyway," I said, "that's not what I was thinking about. I was thinking about steak. A rare steak, with eggs over easy and really greasy hash browns."

The lawyer was about to do something, start yelling or maybe climb off the roof and get to the side of the boat to throw up, but I didn't wait. As fast as I could I rolled up into a crouch. The man with the cigarette had just inhaled and flicked the butt into the water. He turned when he felt me move, felt me come into a crouch there not two feet away from him. He wasn't ready for that. I ran at him as well as I could and hit him low with my shoulder. I was a bit bigger than he was. I took him pretty well off his feet, and he came down on the gunwale, his feet tangled, grabbing with his arms and going over the side into the water. The one in the salon with Julia was yelling, but I wasn't thinking about that too much.

The gun muzzle was almost against my chest when Sandolin started squeezing off. The safety was still on. He panicked, fumbling with the gun. I got in close and brought both my palms down hard, boxing his ears. He yelped and dropped the gun, and I got my hands behind his neck and pulled him off the cabin. He fell down over the edge of the roof, straight down to where the steep stairs into the salon began. I pushed him, and he fell backward down the companionway on top of the man coming up. I got on my knees and picked up the gun, clicked off the safety. The man who had been down below popped his head up over the top of the stairs and then dropped back down out of sight. I moved into the edge of the companionway door, made sure I could see Julia, and then let go. The gun was a full automatic, and that took me by surprise. It almost jumped out of my hands.

It was like a red spring welling up in the back of the man trying to climb and crawl over the lawyer, trying to get forward toward the V-berth, *thuk-thuk-thuk-thuk,* and the man stopped moving. Sandolin was looking behind him, looking wildly for Julia's pistol. *Thuk-thuk-thuk,* and the lawyer had his own spring flowing and blooming out of his side through his green Polo shirt.

I started running, scrambling from the cockpit onto the cabin roof, past the mast and up to the bow. The man in the water was climbing up the opposite side of the Scarab, ducking down when he saw me. He wasn't my concern just now.

I felt fine then, not dizzy or tired, not thinking in any way you could call thinking, but moving and moving very fast, feeling every part of me working together and doing just fine. The man inside the Scarab wasn't coming out. It was a hole, and he was an animal like me, one animal down in his hole and another up above in sunlight. I had to assume he had the other rifle. If he came out I would kill him; if I went in, he might kill me. The other guy was staying in the water. I couldn't see him, but I didn't have to worry about him; he was unarmed.

As I was about to step onto the bow of the Scarab, I stopped. I went backward, all the way back to the cockpit, watching the door of the bow compartment. I put the rifle down quickly, picked up a box from the seat in the cockpit, and heaved it through the blue air as hard as I could throw. Before it came down I had the rifle back in my hands.

The box landed with a bang near a big square hatch that was screwed shut. Almost as soon, a burst of rifle fire came from inside the compartment, and fiberglass popped and splintered all around the hatch. Then it stopped, and I let things get quiet. After a moment the man inside the compartment yelled a name: "Luis."

If Luis was the one in the water, he wasn't yelling back.

"Tomás!" he hollered.

Everything got quiet, and nothing happened, but I was pretty sure what was about to. I waited for it to come, all ready for it.

He came out the door of the compartment yelling as loud as I've heard a man yell. He turned the rifle to point it back over the top of the Scarab's bow. He was hoping I was there, but as he turned he caught sight of me tucked down in the sailboat's stern. He tried to readjust everything he was doing, yelling and trying to aim but firing wide. I rose up, rising forever it seemed, and firing at the same time he did, *thuk-thuk* — just enough — and he went down in a clatter. I shot him again, *thuk-thuk,* making sure he was gone. As I had risen up from the cockpit I saw why the other man, the man in the water, hadn't yelled back at the one I had shot. He was swimming away toward the south, and he was a long way off. I let him keep swimming.

I went down into the salon and found a knife in the galley to cut Julia free. I found her blouse and helped her put it on and got her on her feet. The side of her face was red. She rubbed her hands and wrists until the color came back into them. We were both breathing hard. She sat down on the quarter berth rubbing her hands and looked at the two men on the floor. She got up and stepped between them and tore open one of the boxes that was left on the table. She ripped at the plastic and took out as much money as she could hold and sat back down on the quarter berth and sort of rubbed at the money, looking up at me and then back down at the money. A few of the bills fell into her lap, but she kept most of it in her hands.

There were two or three inches of seawater sloshing around on the floor. It was coming in through the bullet holes in the hull. She got up, took one of the boxes from the table, and climbed the companionway stairs. I took another and followed her up and out into sunlight.

• • •

IT WAS A FINE, wild way to travel, I thought later on, after I had patched the holes in the top of the bow compartment with duct tape and sluiced the blood out through the scuppers. After I had dumped the dead guy and his gun over the side of the Scarab and picked up the shell casings from the deck. After I had motored over to the man who had been trying to swim away and who was now just treading water in the purple swells. After I had untied the dinghy from the sinking sailboat and left it adrift for him. A fine way to travel, doing forty knots in a cherry red speedboat stuffed with money and shot full of holes, running for the Keys in broad daylight and taking sips from a bottle of Haitian rum we'd found under the big padded console. It was noon when we tied up to the dock and went inside the dentist's house and fell asleep in the enormous bed, exhausted, holding each other close in the half-light with all our clothes still on, waiting for nightfall to come and cover us, blue shadows playing on the walls of the quiet house.

25

I WAS LISTENING to her voice in the other room before I realized I was awake. She was saying all right, yes, midnight, then something about a freeway exit, a gas station. Then she stopped talking. I reached under the bed for the gun and walked into the living room. She was there with her legs drawn up in the armchair looking past the aquarium and out the window.

"Tell me you didn't just make a phone call on a land line."

"I didn't," she said. "I found a cell phone on the boat. I found it because it rang a couple of times. And no, I didn't answer it." She waited, looking at me. "That was Jack. He's out."

"What do you mean he's out?"

"Of the hospital. They put him on a gurney and took him downstairs for an X-ray. The FBI guy who was watching him went down the hall to take a leak, and Jack walked out the door and got in a cab. He wants us to pick him up in Miami."

"And what? Take him to a Dolphins game?"

"He wants to go with us. He says he has some documents we'll need. Social Security cards, drivers' licenses. Where's Etna Furnace?"

"Kentucky, a few miles back from the river. Near Salyersville. Christ, is that where he wants to go?"

She nodded. "He says there's a place we can rest up."

"We need to start loading the money."

"I did it already."

I was surprised, but it was true. When I went outside and opened the trailer it was almost filled with powdered-milk boxes. I checked the leaf springs and the tires on the trailer and they seemed OK. The bow compartment of the Scarab was empty. I stood there in the cool darkness next to the dock and smiled a little, thinking how Dennis the Dentist would scratch his head that weekend when he showed up and saw what his sailboat had turned into.

• • •

THE TRAILER and the big Buick took up five spaces in the parking lot of the Gold Rush Motel, but there were plenty of empty spaces. It was a walk-up clientele. There were two black guys leaning on the railing of the balcony that ran around three sides of the parking lot, and a third black guy out on Biscayne Boulevard arguing with a white hooker.

It's odd, the things you remember; the things that come back to you and the things that don't. Odd how memories attach themselves to very particular, concrete things. Going up the stairs I didn't remember going up them before, until I noticed a heart someone had drawn in the cement while it was curing, with two sets of initials inside the heart, and an arrow. The motel had changed its name and undergone a minor face-lift, and anyway still looked like half the other fleabag flophouses on the boulevard, but it wasn't. It was a very specific motel, and I had been here before. I could remember everything now, the whole thing. More of it than I wanted to, anyway. We went upstairs to the landing, watching the two black guys watching us, and walked into the room, and it was the same room.

Fontana was lying on the bed watching the news on TV. His face was very pale, and he was breathing hard. Julia went to him and kissed him on the forehead and touched his cheek.

I looked out between brown drapes. The two guys were still on the balcony looking at the car and the trailer. Fontana clicked off the TV.

"What are we using for wheels?"

I told him.

"Sounds OK."

A manila envelope lay on the bed.

"Go ahead and pass those out," Fontana said.

I did. New drivers' licenses, new passports, new Social Security cards. He must have done it weeks ago, and I had to say, it was pretty impressive. The various pieces of identification had even been weathered a bit so as not to seem too new. Julia looked hers over and put them in her purse.

"Congratulations," Fontana said. "I wasn't sure you'd actually pull it off. The pickup."

"Well, we made it back."

"That's a good thing, Matthew, because it looks like you're out of a job."

He nodded at the TV set and clicked the sound back on. Tanel filled the screen, standing outside the administration building at the port with microphones stuck in his face. Paul Lewis stood beside him in a new suit, and when his turn came he said something polished and firm about working closely with the authorities. He said something else reassuring about terrorism and security measures and the cruise industry as a whole. The news anchor identified him as Festival Cruise Lines' new security director. I noticed our Lloyds of London rep standing in the background.

Then an image came on that really made me watch. It was a picture shot from a helicopter, and it showed the *Norwegian Empress* foundering in whitecaps, her stern tipped steeply upward, and the rest of her pitched down in the water. The ship was surrounded by Coast Guard vessels and lifeboats and debris. Another shot, also from the air, showed her going under, the stern disappearing in a rush of foam. It made me catch my breath, then take another deep one. The scale of it was stunning. The ship sank like any other thing would sink in water, but it wasn't supposed to do that. I had never seen something that big sink. I had an impulse to throw something at Fontana.

"Holy shit!" Julia said.

The way to do it is wait till it's right between the jetties, the narrowest point. You do it with some dynamite in the bow, say fifteen pounds. Nothing fancy. Dynamite and sandbags, a directed charge.

"You need to explain this," I demanded.

"It's a long story," said Fontana, "but I can sum it up in two words: insurance fraud."

"That's ridiculous," I said. "That's absurd."

"It's not absurd. You ever try to sell a forty-year-old cruise ship? It's not worth the trouble. You might as well scrap it. Or hire someone to sink it. Tanel had delays and cost overruns on two new ships coming out of the yard in Helsinki. That's all it was about. It's all about capital. It's all about cash flow and debt structure and new acquisitions and margins. It's all about money, Matthew, like it always has been."

"You're telling me Tanel blew up one of his own ships?"

"Yes, with the help of the mysterious October Twenty-eighth Brigade."

"No. It doesn't add up. It would cost him more in cancellations than he could ever collect."

"That blows over, Matthew. People forget. It's been studied. The ship was evacuated, by the way. No civilian casualties."

I laughed. "No. Just Neal Atlee and Carlos Menoyo. And Krystal Purvis. And three DEA agents."

"Neal Atlee and Carlos Menoyo almost blew themselves up rigging the explosives. They were fools, and they knew too much. I never should have used them, but I made a mistake and then I fixed it the only way I could. The DEA agents were something I didn't count on. Look, Tanel knew about the bombing because he set it up. But he didn't know about the money on board.

Miriam Benages knew about the money, but she didn't know about the bombing. The DEA got into the act at the last minute. They didn't know about the money, and they didn't know about Tanel's insurance scam. All they knew, or thought they knew, was that they had gotten Miriam Benages to flip for them. They were going to cruise down to the islands with her and finger a big important Cali connection and then make some highly dramatic bust that would help out the agency when budget time rolled around. Let me tell you what was really going to happen. Benages was going to pull a vanishing act on the DEA, right after your three precious agents got gunned down in the street in Grand Cayman. They were dead men already; we just sped up the film a little.

"I'm sorry I made some mistakes, but guess what? I forgive myself. Like I said, it was just about money. The difference is who wound up with the swag this time. It's over now. By the time anyone sorts it out, if they ever do, you'll be long gone. So congratulations. How does it feel?"

He looked at me, waiting.

"No," he said. "You don't want it to be over. You don't want to let go of anything and move on." He paused. "I'll tell you a story, Julia."

"Don't," I said.

"Once upon a time, Matthew was working a big investigation right here in our wicked city. A very complex investigation that was probably not the thing a grief-stricken alcoholic should be working on. At any rate, one strand of the whole mess involved trying to arrest a legendary doper in a motel room. Some bullshit informant told somebody this kingpin was going to be sitting in the motel room at such and such a time. As if people at the top of pyramids do that. As if things worked that way.

"Matthew decides he doesn't want to just hang out in the office for this one. He wants to be the star of the show, put the cuffs on the mystery doper, whose name isn't even known, who's like some ghost in the machine. You see, Julia, Matthew actually believes in good and evil. In the worldly embodiment of evil. And he's talked himself into believing that this particular drug baron is evil incarnate. He's been a supervisor for five years, sitting behind a desk, but he thinks the thing to do is suit up in black and lead the squad into the motel room.

"Oh, I almost forgot. A couple of rookies got the search warrant from a federal judge in the middle of the night, and their supervisor forgot to double-check it.

"The entry team comes up the stairs, eight guys in full battle gear, and rams the door off its hinges. The wrong door. *That* door."

He pointed at the door.

"Matthew is the first one through. He's got a penlight on the barrel of his gun. What he sees isn't what he expects to see. A guy and a girl in bed together. Imagine waking up in the night in a sleazebag motel on Biscayne Boulevard and someone's breaking down the door. The guy reaches to grab something on the bedside table. Matthew sees a glint of metal in the beam of his flashlight. He's drunk. Or he's hung over. He puts a bullet through the kid's head. Later on — a lot later on — I believe he did some research on the young lovers. This was right before Matt thought up the brilliant idea of getting shitfaced one night and cutting off his own trigger finger with a pair of pinking shears. What he found out is that the kids were both freshman law students at U.M. doing a little slumming. The boy was reaching for his glasses.

"There's one more thing. Matthew wasn't just the first guy through the door. He was the only guy through the door. There wasn't any entry team. At the last minute Matthew had them stand down and roll back to the field office. He decided to fly solo, make the arrest on his own. When things went to shit, my pager started going off. It was Matt, hysterical. Lucky thing I was eight blocks away eating a steak at the 1800 Club. And a lucky thing we had worked a lot of the early parts of the case together on an interagency task force. You can see the rest. Matt and I switched places, and I took the fall for him. It made sense: he had a wife with pancreatic cancer he needed to be there for. If he'd lost his job, she would have lost her medical insurance.

"I almost forgot. The kingpin Matthew was after? He never even found out his name. Partly because it wasn't a he. It was a she. Miriam Benages. How's it feel, Matthew? Fortuna's Wheel, right? Here you sit with thirty million of Miriam's money. She's history, and you're still walking around."

I looked at him for quite a while. Julia got up and whispered something in his ear and went outside, closing the door of the room behind her.

"I'm feeling a tad grumpy," Fontana said.

"No shit. I can tell. How much longer you think you have?"

"Not much. So let's go to Etna Furnace. It's more for you."

"I know. Speaking of which, did you forward any mail to the house up there? Set up new phone service? An account at the power company?"

"Relax, slick. You're a ghost now. You and Julia both. There's no way anyone can trace you from here to there. But look, there's a couple facts I want to hit you with. It's about Julia. Her and you and me. She wanted me to talk to you about some things, and I think you probably want to sit down for this."

"I've got something to tell you, too."

"Fine. You go first. I already know what happened to Kip and Manuel. Jesus. Getting nailed to a cross can fuck up your whole week."

"But you don't know Miriam Benages is alive."

He sat up on the edge of the bed.

"You're joking."

"I'm not. I saw her yesterday morning on Flagler Street."

"Christ. Fuck!"

"Yeah. We gotta go."

I took his hand and helped him stand up and walk over to the door. Downstairs in the parking lot Julia gave us both a big hug.

Fontana settled into the back seat of the Buick. As I drove the car out of the lot, the trailer hitch scraping the pavement, he was saying, "This duck walks into a bar, hops up on a bar stool, and orders a pair of Heinekens. . . ."

26

W E TOOK THE OLD WAY out of town, the way people once came into the city from up north before the turnpike or interstate existed. The way led north and west, a diagonal cutting through Little Havana and then past the edge of Hialeah beside a canal where love motels lined one side of the road. After a long while, when the country opened up, there were miles of sugarcane fields, and then the land changed again and started to roll: hills and lakes, with cattle and citrus and, later still, fancy horse farms with white rail fences.

We crossed the Suwannee River and stopped while Fontana took our picture using a throwaway camera, with Julia and me standing beside a sign that read:

Welcome to Georgia, State of Adventure. We gassed up and kept going, past Valdosta, Tifton, Macon, on the interstate now, coming into the morning sprawl of Atlanta and sleeping a few hours at a Days Inn.

We kept going. Fontana was flying, rambling, his eyes glassy. He would sleep and then wake up and start talking in midsentence, not realizing he had been asleep. We kept going north, past Chattanooga, Knoxville, then the long haul to Lexington, Julia driving until we turned east on I-64 and finally got off the interstate onto 203, bearing north again toward Ironton. The heater had stopped working.

"I'm cold," she said. She nestled into me, and I felt her shaking. I put my arm around her shoulders and drew her against me.

Fontana groaned. She listened for a time, but nothing more came from the backseat.

I felt like talking. "Did you ever look for your real parents?"

She laughed and gave me an odd look. "Last year. Jack helped me. But you know that."

"Jack again."

"Yes. Pull over. I want to check on him."

I stopped, and she got out and opened the back door on her side. She listened to Fontana's chest with the stethoscope. Then she bent down with her ear next to his mouth and adjusted the wadded-up clothes under his head. She got back in the front seat, and I started the engine.

"Wait," she said.

"What?"

"There's something —".

I waited, but she didn't say anything. She was shaking again. I drew her close to me. I waited a little longer, and then I turned and kissed her. She drew back and started to speak, but instead she reached out and took me by the back of the neck, her fingers holding tight to my hair. She looked into my eyes, frowning, and then pulled my face toward her and pressed her lips against mine. This time she was right there with me, not pushing away anymore. I kissed her neck, and her hand moved down over my stomach.

I unbuttoned her blouse, and she pulled me down onto the car seat. I listened for sounds from the back, but Fontana was breathing steadily.

"Hurry," she said. "Go fast."

She had already unbuckled my belt and started pushing my pants down. I ran my hands up the sides of her thighs and tore at her underwear until the elastic broke. She had one arm around my back and the other around my neck, holding my head down next to hers so that I couldn't see her face. Then I was inside her, and then all the way inside her. She grabbed the hair on the back of my head, holding my face down. She tried to wrap her legs around me but there were too many clothes in the way, and her foot kept hitting the steering wheel. "Go fast," she said, and I did.

She arched her back, making a small, high-pitched sound, a moan that went on and rose and became rhythmic. I pulled her back toward me on the seat so her head wouldn't smack against the door. She shifted under me and arched her back again. Then she let go of my hair and put her hands above her, behind her head. I held her wrists down on the seat and sucked on her nipples, first one, then the other, with my eyes closed. Inside me I could see white specks and stars. I could hear her moaning, saying something, but at the same time that I was right there on top of her on the car seat I was a long way off, somewhere else. She had gotten one hand free and had it around the back of my head now, pushing my head down against her breast. Just before everything went red I pulled my head up and away from her and felt myself falling forward. My head hit the window and kept going through the glass, little pieces of safety glass crunching and falling everywhere. She had screamed and turned her head to the side with her eyes closed. I looked down, and she was crying and had been all along. Her face was wet with tears.

"Are you —"

"Don't stop!" she said. "Don't stop!"

I kept going and then everything was red and deeper red, and I heard my own voice and inside a starburst of red I could hear her saying something again and again, crying and holding me as hard as she could and saying something over and over that sounded like *Daddy, Daddy, Daddy*. That's what I remembered later, but right then I wasn't thinking about it. I felt her freeze, and then I froze, too, hearing the noise in the backseat, a choking cough that might have been going on for some time.

She was trying to get out from underneath me, and I was trying to help her. She got her legs free and got the door open, glass crunching and falling when she opened it. She pulled the rear door open and tore the clothes away from under his head. For a moment I thought she was kissing him, but of course she was trying to make him breathe. She kept tilting his head back, one hand on his chin, another behind his head, breathing in and putting her mouth to his and then breathing into him. She stopped and put her head down on his chest, her hair falling over his face. Then she shoved at his chest, surprisingly hard. She was crying while she did it, tears running down her face and down her breasts. Her nipples stayed erect in the cold, and she was shaking. I got in the other side and straddled him on the backseat, and when she went back to blowing air into him I pumped at his chest. I would pump ten times, and she would breathe into him, and I would go back to pumping. We kept going and going, and it was a rhythm now.

He never opened his eyes. After a long time she started crying again, listening to his chest and then kissing his forehead, her hands cradling his head. Finally she stood up and put on her blouse and buttoned it, still crying. I got out of the backseat and closed the door and walked around to her side of the car.

"It's snowing," she said, wiping her face.

I looked, and it was. I hadn't seen snow in ten years. It was coming down so softly in the darkness, the snowflakes glinting and disappearing in silence, white in the black night.

27

I HAD NOTICED the car in the distance coming toward us but I had my back to it, facing Julia. While I watched her she stopped crying, and her face went blank. She turned away from me with a jerk and reached into the front seat of the car as I looked behind me at the cruiser with its blue lights flashing, pulling over onto the shoulder and coming to a stop a few feet behind the U-Haul.

The state trooper was going to be young, I was sure of that. I knew it before he got out of the car. He had pulled up too close to the trailer, blocking his own view of the Buick. When he opened his door and started getting out, I was even more sure of it; he got out too fast. If he had used the radio at all, it was only to give his location to the dispatcher. He hadn't run the license plate. It was an out-of-state plate and would have taken longer than usual. And it was almost midnight, the end of a shift. This was probably his last stop, and not one he had expected to make. He got out of the cruiser, bringing his hat with him, and he was very young.

I tried to think about what he was seeing: a middle-aged guy in jeans and a sweatshirt who had just walked over and leaned against the rear door on the driver's side and folded his arms. A young woman standing on the other side of the car, shivering in the night breeze. Neither one dressed for the cold.

"How y'all doin'?" he asked, approaching me. "Everything all right?"

"Just stopped to stretch our legs," I said. "How's it going?"

"Fine," he said. "Ma'am," he added, giving Julia a good looking over. She didn't say anything. "Kind of a bad place to be pulled over at," he said, glancing into the front seat of the car. "You mind if I look at your license and proof of insurance?"

"Oh, sure." I shifted getting my wallet out, and he saw there was something in there beyond the rear window. He took a step back and reached to unsnap his holster. He was left-handed.

"What is that in your backseat, sir?"

"A real sick man, officer. My brother."

"Could you ask him to step out of the car, sir?"

"I could, but I don't think he'd be able to. In fact, we were thinking of taking him in to the nearest hospital. He seems like he's taken a turn for the worse."

I was sure the trooper was thinking about his cruiser, wishing he had stayed in it a little longer. I wondered if he had noticed the shattered front window yet.

"Folks," he said, "I'm going to ask both of you to step up in front of your car there, a few feet in front of it, and just wait there for a minute."

"No problem," I said.

When we were standing in front of the car, he reached inside the Buick and turned on the headlights. I could see him giving the front seat of the car a careful look. I remembered the gun in the glove compartment. Then I heard the glove compartment thump open and heard it close again a moment later, as though there hadn't been anything interesting for him to see inside it.

He opened the back door. It was a full minute, more than a minute, before he closed it again, and then he didn't close it all the way, but just sort of settled it shut.

"Sir," he said, "I'm going to ask you to come and get in the backseat of the patrol car, if you would, please. You wait right there, ma'am."

It was the first good idea he'd had, but he was going to

screw it up, too. On the way to the cruiser, me walking ahead of him, he paused at the doors of the trailer and put his hand on the stock of his holstered pistol.

"Do you mind showing me what you have inside this trailer?"

"Is there something wrong, officer?"

"No, nothing wrong. Would you show me what's in there?"

"Not without a search warrant."

"Oh," he said after a moment.

"Just joking." I reached for the handle and unbolted the doors and swung them open.

The trooper looked at the cardboard cartons inside.

"What is that?"

"It's powdered condensed milk."

He thought about that.

"Open one up for me, would you, sir?"

I had been buying time, but I was going broke fast. I looked down, watching his pale, smallish hand resting on the top of the gun.

"Sir?" he said.

I opened one of the cardboard boxes and held it up. When he saw what was inside, packed tight in the clear plastic, he took his gun out of the holster.

Then he was raising his pistol very quickly with a startled look on his face under the round, broad-brimmed hat. Julia had come around the side of the trailer so quietly I hadn't heard her until the last moment. She was holding the gun straight out in both hands.

The muzzle flash blinded me for an instant, but not before I saw the trooper's head snap back, his hat falling off. I had grabbed the gun, grabbed her wrist so hard the gun fell from her hand. As I did it I saw the trooper start backward into the road, his pistol falling from his fingers, clattering, and his head hitting the pavement with a dull, wet smack. Julia had tripped and sat down, pulling me down with her onto my knees.

"No!" I screamed into her face. "No!"

I slapped her. She looked shocked and then began to cry and try to tear away from me. I grabbed her by the arms and shook her.

"I didn't have a choice!" she cried.

"You always have a choice. Always!"

She pushed hard against me and wrenched herself away. She got up and walked over to the cruiser and half sat against its hood.

• • •

I WASN'T SURE it was worth doing, but I was doing it. We had to expect roadblocks and checkpoints, media saturation, extra state police and sheriff's deputies going to alpha-bravo shifts to solve a cop shooting, and it was all going to happen fast. Doing what I was doing might slow it down, delay it. But it was costing time in the meanwhile.

There was a boat ramp about five miles back the way we had come, marked with a sign, an emblem of a fish and a fishhook. She stayed a quarter mile behind me in the Buick while I drove the cruiser.

It was a paved road off the four-lane highway, and I was grateful for that. It meant no trace of tire tracks. The radio crackled once, a dispatcher calling out to the trooper in the trunk. I turned the radio off and tried not to think about the young woman in the photo clipped on the little gooseneck notepad holder that stuck out from the dashboard next to the steering wheel. She had an engagement ring on her hand.

The land dropped steadily through dense, wet forest, the access road going straight down to the edge of the Ohio River. I pulled into an empty parking lot with extra-long spaces for cars with trailers. There was one dim light on a post between two concrete boat ramps. Julia pulled in and parked but didn't get out.

I popped the trunk on the cruiser and looked inside, holding the trooper's flashlight. The trooper stirred and groaned. Then he opened his eyes. He looked at me for a time before his eyes focused.

"Am I shot?"

"You're shot in the hat," I said.

"What happened?"

"You tripped and hit your head. Come on, try to stand up and get out of the trunk."

I held the gun on him while he struggled to sit up and then climbed out of the trunk. He stood beside the car with his hands cuffed behind him, shivering.

I led him back into the woods the better part of two hundred yards, bringing one of the blankets from the Buick and a rain poncho from the patrol car.

"Sit down. I'm going to handcuff your foot to that tree root you see right there. It's just for a few hours. I'll call dispatch first thing in the morning and have someone pick you up."

When he was sitting down on the poncho, I unlocked the cuffs and freed his hands and then locked the cuffs again, one ring around his ankle, the other around the root of the tree. I draped the blanket over his shoulders and set his hat on the ground beside him.

He picked up the hat and stuck his finger through the bullet hole in the crown.

"Souvenir, I guess."

"I guess. How's your head?"

He touched the back of his scalp and looked at his hand. It was too dark for him to see if there was blood on it.

"Seems OK."

"All right. I'm off then."

As I was backing away he said, "Could I ask you a favor?"

"Go on."

"Today's my birthday. My girlfriend's making fried chicken."

"You mean your fiancée."

"Yeah. I'm not used to saying it that way. My fiancée. She's making fried chicken."

"You want me to call her."

"She's going to really worry."

I hesitated, then walked over and pointed the gun at him and took the pen out of his breast pocket.

"What's her number?"

He told me. I knelt, keeping my distance, and put the gun and the flashlight on the wet earth and wrote the numbers on the palm of my hand, glancing at him while I did it.

•　　•　　•

I WALKED BACK through the woods to the boat ramp
and stood beside some riprap, watching a big barge out
on the river fighting north against the current. Even
near the riverbank the water moved along swiftly, and
that helped what I was going to do.

I made sure all the windows were closed in the cruiser
and got it near the slope of the boat ramp, then drove
with the door open and one foot skimming the concrete
outside, giving it plenty of gas, and jumped out of the car
as it hit the ramp. I had managed to slam the door shut
as I bailed out and slid and sat down hard.

The engine compartment sank, the car nose down,
but the rest of the cruiser stuck up in the air. There
was enough momentum to carry it out into the current.
It rotated slowly while it bubbled and sank.

28

THE HOUSE WAS wood frame and looked down into
a hollow from a hill behind a crossroads where
cars never came anymore. At the crossroads was the
tumbled-down bulk of what had been a gas station and
general store. Along that side of the road, farther on,
were half a dozen shacks even worse off than the store,
and a big slag heap dusted with early-winter snow. More
recently someone had brought in a house trailer, but it
was burned out and empty now.

A road left the cracked pavement and ran up over the
hill. From the house you could see anyone who ap-
proached, but no one could see the house from the crossroads. Here and there, if you knew where to look, were
holes in the sides of hills, doorways into the earth made

for getting out the coal. All the machinery from the mines was long gone.

The cutoff that led back to the big blast furnace had grown over until it was nothing more than a path through thick woods. I had looked around here one day after coming home from overseas, looked at the furnace that even then was covered in vines. There had been an uncle who came out to the mailbox by the road to talk. He lived in the house for some years after my father was gone and had the idea of putting up siding that looked like brick from a distance. The fake brick siding had come loose over the years, and now it flapped in the wind. There were various outbuildings: an old stable with a hayloft, once used for mules and now a tractor barn and toolshed; the remains of an outhouse; the smokehouse, its roof fallen in.

The house might have made a good place for a stand-off, but the more I thought about it and where it was, it seemed like a bad place to hide. Behind it the land dropped through woods to a broad rocky creek that ran full in winter. A railroad line followed the creek along its far bank. It was through these woods and across the deep creek that someone would have to travel to get out of the place if he couldn't get out the front way. It was no one's idea of a good escape route.

If it were up to me I would have left the next day, but

that was impossible. Julia would go outside and listen to the car radio and come back with what they had said about the young trooper and the roadside shooting. There was no way we were leaving there for at least a week, until things cooled down.

The only heat was from a kerosene stove in the main room. I would wake up at night hearing the train whistle and then hear her moving around the house in the darkness or standing next to a window, looking out through a gap in the makeshift curtains we had put up. The baby-food jar sat on the table, half full of white powder. She would go to it, help herself to more of it, and be even more certain she had heard something or someone outside. I unloaded the two handguns and put them under the kitchen sink.

That first night, I had backed the trailer into the low stable and uncoupled it from the car. Then, after I'd gotten the stove going in the house, I put a shovel in the backseat of the car and took the car down the lane to where the path went through the woods to the blast furnace.

After it was done, I stood around blowing on my hands and tried to think of something to say, a prayer, but I couldn't. In the end I said, "Well, we've wound up where we started," thinking he'd laugh at that. I made my way around the furnace and pushed apart bushes here and there looking for the brick we had scratched our initials on when we were kids, but I couldn't find it. Coming back I discovered a chunk of rotting wood I could tell was full of foxfire and would glow in the night. I left it for him, thinking that was pretty good, really.

When I came back she didn't say anything. The next day she wanted to know where he was buried but wouldn't walk down there and look at the grave. She stayed in the house, as far from me as she could, hardly speaking, not eating. I wished I had talked more with her about what Fontana meant in her life. I didn't understand it, and now, with her like she was, it wasn't the time to ask. And so it went. Two weeks passed, then three.

One morning I heard her in the bathroom, what sounded like coughing or choking, and sobbing. She was in there for a long time after the sounds stopped, and when she came out her eyes were red. She walked past me and lay down on the pallet next to the kerosene stove and pulled a quilt over her head.

I waited until the afternoon light was fading before we started down the mountain in the car. She still wasn't talking, but I thought she had begun to relax a bit by the time we reached the outskirts of the town. At one point I glanced at her and saw she was studying the calendar on the inside cover of her checkbook. She saw me watching her and put the checkbook away and turned toward the window.

The town was getting ready for a big Saturday night. Away from the old downtown business section there were bright lights shining down on the parking lot of a shopping plaza and young guys in pickups cruising past with their girls. I found a place that sold kerosene and then discovered it was no longer a dry county and bought cigarettes and a bottle of bourbon and two bags of ice. We still needed kerosene to heat the house, but there was plenty of light in the darkness now; in the middle of the second night I had woken up to a blaze of lamps and the rattle of a broken ceiling fan. The power had come on, and I knew Jack had arranged it, no doubt long before we left Miami. The next day I picked up the telephone in the hallway and heard a dial tone, and it made me even more uneasy. The phone and the lights were connections to the outer world I didn't want. They were a scent, a footprint in the snow, if you knew how to use them — a way to track us.

Days before, Julia had found my uncle's longbow and a quiver of hunting arrows hanging on the wall in the stable. They were the remains of a fad, and I remembered he had used the bow for only a season or two before going back to his rifle. On the way out of town I stopped at a sporting goods store and found a new bow-string, thinking this might get her going, give her some-thing to focus on. I bought some cedar target arrows so she wouldn't have to use the old aluminum ones with their heavy broadhead tips. The four-bladed broadheads were rusty but still razor sharp and not something any-one civilized really wanted to look at. Next we parked in front of a grocery store, but a pair of police cruisers was idling side to side, the cops talking, and we decided to keep driving.

Later, when the train whistle woke me up, and I was sure she was asleep, I crept into the bathroom, closed the door softly, and turned on the light. At the bottom of the wastebasket, underneath some tissue paper, a green-and-white box looked up at me. On its side it had a car-toon stork with a bundle in its beak and a picture of a happy man and woman, embracing. The woman was holding up a little stick, a test strip, for the man to examine.

29

THE NEXT DAY I woke up and she was gone. I had poured some coffee and walked outside to a stump and worked my way through two dozen chunks of oak with the splitting maul, trying to believe the car would come up the road with Julia in it and I would help her unload groceries. After half an hour I went around to the stable and checked on the money. About half of it was missing, along with the trailer.

The edge of a white envelope stuck out from between two powdered-milk boxes. I opened it and pulled out a sheet of paper. It was a photocopy of a birth certificate. The copy had been copied many times over, but the grainy print was clear enough. The words at the top said Florida State Board of Health. My wife's name and signature were near the bottom, along with my name, typed in, and the date, November 11, 1976. The child had been a girl: Julia. Julia Shannon. *I hereby certify that this child was born alive on the date stated above;* next to that a doctor's signature.

I sat down on the dirt floor of the stable, seeing myself in a memory saying, *"You remind me of someone I used to know."* Pull over, she had said, there's something — something she had needed to tell me. I held the paper in my hand until it started to blur and I couldn't make it out anymore. I knew at some point I was going to have to stand up again, so after another minute I just went ahead and did it, taking a step forward and then another, walking out of the stable, still holding the piece of paper in my hand.

I spent the rest of the morning putting the cash in garbage bags and burying it in the woods near some big rocks about a hundred yards from the house. When I spread pine needles over the spot it looked just like everywhere else, and I figured it would do until I thought of a better idea.

The two handguns were still under the sink where I had hidden them, but she had taken my uncle's hunting bow with her. For a while I sat at the kitchen table and looked out the window. It was very quiet. I got the bottle down from the shelf and poured a drink. Something moved at the edge of the woods, and then a medium-size doe stepped out into the sunlight with her fawn. I sat still and watched them nuzzle around in the grass and walk back into the trees, taking their time.

While I walked down the mountain I looked for deer tracks, and there were plenty of them. I noticed some others that might have been coyote. Tomorrow morning I would split the rest of the wood, but right now I was hungry, and I also wanted to see about a car. There was a restaurant in town, Scotty's Spot, that served a mean steak. Scotty's Spot was a thousand miles from Florida, but one of the items on the menu was Key lime pie. You can have anything in this country if you want it bad enough, something my old man used to say. I tried to imagine him standing at a crossroads mining camp called Etna Furnace and actually believing that.

It was five miles to town, and by the time I got there I had stopped crying and begun to wonder if there was a place in the world for someone who wanted to split white-oak blocks all morning and look for coyote tracks in the afternoon. Then I laughed at all that and cussed for quite a little while, and before long I heard a pair of birds calling out to each other, and soon I began to sing a bit myself.

· · ·

BUT YOU KNOW how it is. I got down there, and they had run out of Key lime pie. I ordered a slice of lemon chess instead, and while I was eating it I thought about the coyote tracks, and then I was thinking about a guy I arrested one time in a lemon grove. I didn't know a lot about animals, but I had learned some things about people, how they move and behave, how to track them. I had been pretty good at that.

She wouldn't leave a credit-card trail, and she would be smart enough to stick to secondary roads. I thought I knew what direction she had taken: west, the way so many skips did, and had, for so many years, maybe from the early days of the country. There was something about it; following the sun, I suppose.

I took my time walking through town and picking out a five-year-old Chevy at a car lot. The guy seemed happy enough for me to pay in small bills. On the way out of town I stopped to gas up and clean out the car a bit.

I started thinking about the money, the money under the ground. I already had a shopping-bag-full stashed in the trunk. But I started thinking it might not be enough. What if I didn't catch up to her in a few days? What if it was a month? It might be smart to take some more money, because there was no telling when I might get back here. I had nothing but time, after all. There was no reason to be in a hurry. That's what I was thinking.

That's what I was thinking when I looked across the street from the gas station and saw a blue van sitting there with its engine running. It was the kind of van that has a bulky contraption rigged up to the back of it for someone who's handicapped, someone who needs to get around in a wheelchair. A dark guy was in the driver's seat looking at me, his hands on the wheel. And the way the van was parked, the way the street was laid out at an oblique angle to the gas station, I could see the shape of someone beyond and beside him, a smaller shape sitting next to the driver there in the passenger seat, not moving but waiting, her hand playing with a crucifix on a chain.

And right at that moment Julia pulled up to one of the gas pumps in the Buick, got out and unscrewed the gas cap, and then saw me and smiled and started running toward me. She bent her head down through the window and kissed me on the lips.

"I'm sorry," she said. "I'm sorry I ran. I was scared. But I'm back. I came back. Everything's all right now."

The blue van sat there. No one had gotten out. The man in the passenger seat watched us. I looked at the Buick and saw the trailer was missing.

"Julia — where's the trailer?"

She looked hurt for a moment. "Don't worry. I hid it in a safe place. I thought it was better than driving back here with it."

"Good," I heard myself say. "That's very good. I'm glad you did that. It was very smart to do that."

"Did you get what I left you?"

I didn't know what she meant. Then I did — the piece of paper in the envelope. The birth certificate. I nodded.

"I thought you'd like to have a little evidence after your conversation with Jack," she said.

"Let's wait and talk about it after a while."

The guy in the van took his hands off the steering wheel. He lay his left arm along the open window and looked at me.

"Hey, are you OK? You're shaking."

"I'm fine," I said. "I'm just so happy to see you. But look, I need you to do something —"

"Matthew," she said. "You did talk to Jack, didn't you? In the motel room? Back in Miami?"

I tried to think. "There was something he said he wanted to tell me, but we didn't get around to it."

She was starting to cry.

"There's more than what you know," she said. "It's about Jack. Your wife and Jack. They had something going once. They had an affair, a long time ago. In 1976."

"What?" I didn't understand what she was saying.

"You asked me what I was to him. He's — he was —

my father. Not you. Your name's on the birth certificate, but he was my father. Why do you keep looking over there?" She turned and looked past the gas pumps at the van on the other side of the street. Then she turned back, worried.

"Did Jack tell you all this?" I asked.

"No. She did. Before she died. I saw her in the hospital. Jack took me to see her."

She was still standing outside the car window. I put my hand on her arm. She tried to laugh, touching my cheek and saying, Don't cry, baby. I've never seen you do that. It's going to be fine now. We'll do everything together.

I was trying to think as hard as I could, think how it was going to be fine, and the only thing I could think of was half a plan. I had to separate them, and I thought I knew how.

"I need you to do something," I said. "I need you to leave here right now, pay for your gas and just drive out of town and keep going as fast as you can go. I'll meet you in L.A. next week. I'll be right behind you. There's a hotel near the big pier in Santa Monica, the Loews. You check in and wait for me."

"Who's in that van, Matthew? Who is it? Please."

"It's nobody, just an old friend who's going to set me up with a few things we'll need later on."

"Another disguise?" She laughed.

"Maybe," I said, winking. "Maybe some of your favorite white powder, too. The thing of it is, she'll get nervous if you're involved. She's already wondering what's going on over here. Please, just do this for me. You drive away first, and I'll follow right behind you. You'll see me turn off at the house, but you keep going. Keep going, and we'll have plenty of time later to talk about everything. I can't explain any more. You have to go now and do it just like I said."

"I'm pregnant."

"I know that. It'll be fine."

"Look me in the eyes," she said. "Promise me you'll be in L.A. next week. Promise. I'll know if you're lying."

I looked in her eyes, pale gray with flecks of gold around the pupils.

"I promise."

I let go of her, and she went inside and paid for the gas. She came back out, not looking at me, and got in the Buick and pulled out of the gas station. I moved into the street right behind her.

She drove slowly out of town and then gained speed when the town fell away and the land opened up. I stayed close on her, watching the van coming along behind me in the rearview mirror a few hundred feet back.

We got near the side road that turned off the highway.

I put my turn signal on and started slowing down. There was a moment when she touched her brakes, but then she kept going, picking up speed again and finally disappearing around a curve.

I turned onto the gravel road. Sweat had come up on my hands and face. The road climbed steadily up to a bench, giving me a good view of the highway back behind me. The van had slowed down and stopped at the turnoff. Then, very slowly, it started moving onto the side road, leaving the highway behind and coming along on the wet gravel up through an old apple orchard.

I drove back up the mountain to the house, parked, and walked into the woods to the big rocks. I got all the way there and realized I'd forgotten the shovel, so I walked back and got it and started digging. After a few minutes I took off my shirt and lit a cigarette, and when I'd smoked it, I started digging again.

I turned when I heard her rack the slide on the shotgun. She was between two big pine trees, sitting in the wheelchair with the dark guy standing behind her. The next thing was the blue morning air exploding, shattering. Then I was sitting down. At first I couldn't breathe, and then I could, and I could feel my heart beating fast. She wheeled herself out of the trees with the man's help and came to within fifteen feet of me. Her eyes were always the same — the same two black stones sunk in her fleshy face. Two wet black stones in a mountain stream. She didn't look angry or hateful at all, just curious, waiting.

There had been a buzzing sound inside my head, and now it became a roar. My hands were gently touching at the wet stuff in my lap. I looked down at them until they seemed like someone else's hands. I couldn't make them stop playing and poking at what was there in my lap and spilling onto the ground. Gutshot, I thought, but the word didn't seem any more real than what I was looking at.

I thought about my wife, and then I thought about her, Julia. I had been pretty sure she would go west and that I could pick up her trail. Get to her and explain things before — before what? And what things?

I had an image of myself driving cross-country at night, the desert country I hadn't seen in years. It had rained, and I could smell sage through the open window. I was happy because I was going to find her. Then I had another image: two cars stopped beside the road, me walking toward her in starlight. Then she was in my arms, and I was holding her, telling her everything would be all right.

But maybe I never would have found her. Maybe what had happened was all that could have happened. Anyway, I felt like I had been figuring things out pretty well there at the end. Starting to, at least. I had gotten the fever back a little, the old forward motion, going toward something.

Then all at once it felt like the whole world had stopped moving. Of course, I knew it was only me.

I must have been gone and then come back, awake, hearing a twig snap, or what I thought was a twig; the *slap-crack* of great tension held for a long, long time and suddenly released. I looked up and saw the dark guy turn and stagger to one side, both his hands clutching the stick that had grown from his chest. He moved in a slow, sleepwalker's circle, his mouth open to the sky, and I had the odd thought that if it started raining, his mouth would fill up with water. He came back to where he had started his shuffling dance and fell on the ground, bringing his knees up to his chest. But I wasn't looking at him anymore. I was looking at Miriam Benages. I watched her eyes turn to one side and then the other in a wondering sort of way, then finally look up at the aluminum shaft that stuck out a foot and a half from the center of her forehead, the four blades of the broadhead forming a perfect cross.

Julia moved up through the woods toward the wheelchair with the longbow in her hand. The winter light fell down through the pines and lit up her eyes, and I heard the thrum of a woodpecker somewhere nearby and high up. Then it was the way I had always felt watching my wife walk through any doorway. It was like watching the sun rise over a landscape I had never known. Her gray eyes looked straight into mine, and I was rising now myself, getting one foot under me and trying to come up, fighting. She didn't smile, but I could imagine her smiling again somewhere in the times to come, walking along a street or standing in a market-place, maybe in another country. She had a third arrow nocked against the bowstring, just in case we needed it.

ACKNOWLEDGMENTS

Wherein the author advertises gratitude for his three favorite lit chicks: Christine Tague, first reader, ace copyeditor, and loyal friend; Judy Clain of Little, Brown and Company, editrix extraordinaire; and literary agent Sarah Burnes, without whom I would still be sleeping in my truck.

ABOUT THE AUTHOR

Sean Rowe has been a reporter for the *Miami Herald* and senior writer for the *Miami New Times*. He lives in North Carolina, where he is renovating a turn-of-the-century farmhouse and working on his next novel. Learn more about the author at www.sean-rowe.com.